# TWINKLE, TWINKLE, DEADLY SPRINKLES

## AN IVY CREEK COZY MYSTERY

RUTH BAKER

CLEANTALES PUBLISHING

# AN IVY CREEK COZY MYSTERY

## BOOK TWO

It was a sunny afternoon, and the birds chirping in the sky above reminded Lucy of a time when she played on the patio while her parents worked in the bakery. She had grown up happy, her hours spent learning recipes from her mother's cookbook, and holidays full of entertaining events like the summer kid's camp and marathon races. Those fond memories she held on to filled her leisure time.

She sighed when the door behind her opened, and Hannah, her employee and friend, walked out, holding two glasses.

"Freshly made orange juice," Hannah said, smiling as Lucy took a glass.

"Thanks," Lucy replied, and took a sip. Hannah settled into a chair close to Lucy's and took out a notepad from her apron's pocket. "Have you made a list of the needed items?"

Hannah pushed the notepad to Lucy. "We have a week to the delivery date, so we should get them tomorrow, and then we begin preparations."

She had made great sales since the bakery reopened, and

there were more to come. She was certain of it. Lucy took out a pen from her shirt pocket and scribbled down additional flavors.

She was trying out a new recipe and if she perfected it in time, it would be a new addition for their menu. "Thank you, Hannah," she said, after making the notes.

Hannah placed both her hands on the table, and Lucy sipped her juice as she turned to her friend.

"Have you heard?" Hannah asked, clearing her throat.

Hannah was Lucy's source for town gossip. She lived downtown, and since Lucy remained in the apartment upstairs, she barely had contact with the citizens of Ivy Creek unless they came to Sweet Delights.

"Heard?"

"About the merger." Hannah's eyes widened as she continued. "It's the talk of the town. *James Anderson* took over a small accounting firm. This is the third time in two years they've taken over some small firm."

Lucy was aware of *James Anderson*, the town's biggest accounting firm owned by Roland Anderson, who belonged to one of the town's founding families. His father had started the company, and they had expanded a lot in the last few years. She had never done business with him, but he had a lot of clout in town.

"Some say his wife got him the deal," Hannah continued. "I think they worked hand in hand on every acquisition, but the glory goes to the husband every time."

As Hannah talked, Lucy spotted a red Mustang approaching. The driver stopped and parked by the corner of the street, and when the door opened, a lady stepped out.

Hannah looked at it, and her jaw dropped. "That's Mrs. Anderson," she announced in a shaky voice, and Lucy saw Hannah's cheeks turn red.

Blushing, Hannah excused herself and scurried into the

bakery. Lucy watched as Mrs. Anderson walked towards the patio with short, calculated steps.

She wore an immaculate white Chanel pantsuit that gave her an exquisite business look and a pair of designer sunglasses that made her look like a Hollywood celebrity. Lucy also did not miss the hot red color of her lipstick. Her black stilettos clicked on the floor with each step she took and made a distinct sound that was hard to ignore.

*The rumors are probably right about her; everything about her exudes wealth,* Lucy thought.

*What were the odds that they were just talking about her and she came here? What did she want?*

Lucy shook the thoughts away and rose to her feet when Mrs. Anderson got to the patio. The subtle scent of magnolia and jasmine reached Lucy's nostrils as Mrs. Anderson slowly took off the shades she wore.

"Hi," she greeted in a silky tone, and extended a hand. "Becky Anderson."

Lucy accepted the extended hand and smiled.

"Lucy, right?" Becky asked, skipping formalities, and Lucy nodded.

"Yes," she replied. She noticed her well-manicured red painted nails and the elaborate stitching on the pantsuit she wore. "Have a seat," she offered, and Becky sat. "Is there something you need?"

Becky smiled. The corners of her lips curved, and the sides of her eyes wrinkled. "Of course, dear," she replied. "I wouldn't drive all the way out here if I didn't." She glanced at the gold watch on her slender wrist for a second and when she raised her gaze, Lucy met her deep velvety brown eyes.

"My husband and I are hosting a charity event next weekend, and I need services for baked treats," she continued. "I always hire the very best, and I've…" She took a slight pause, and she looked around the patio. "I've heard you're good at what you do," she added.

Becky smiled again. "Are you?"

Lucy chose not to answer the last question. With a deep sigh, she linked her fingers on her lap and replied. "I would like to know what you have in mind for the treats, your budget, and of course, guest list."

Becky reached into her designer purse, took out a piece of paper, and handed it over to Lucy. "I've made a list of everything required of you. It's all written there."

Lucy scanned the notes on the paper and frowned. "There's no budget. A budget plays a role, as it helps us work smoothly," she explained, and dropped the paper. "You should state a budget which, of course, includes my pay for the event."

Lucy raised her chin, determined not to let Becky's intimidating presence bait her. She could handle business deals and she was every bit as professional as Becky Anderson.

Becky chuckled softly. "Like I mentioned earlier, it's a charity event. Surely you know what charity events are?"

"I do…"

"That's great," Becky interrupted. "You offer your services for free, just as I am hosting the event to gather proceedings for charity. My husband and I do this every year, and this year we're trying to raise more… for a good cause."

Lucy pressed her lips together, but Becky remained persistent.

"If you agree to do this, of course you will gain the right amount of publicity for your bakery. As director of the local chamber of commerce, I will have many guests in attendance who are all potential clients of yours with the right recommendation."

Lucy analyzed her offer quietly as she stared at the list of treats needed and the number of guests. *Over two hundred guests meant some were non-locals. It was definitely going to be a major event.*

"I take it you're thinking about my offer," Becky said after a minute of silence. She waved her hand as she continued. "There are a few potential clients on my list I can hand over to you right now once you agree to this deal."

"What's in it for you?" Lucy asked. "Seems like you're offering more than you'll be receiving."

Becky shrugged. "Let's just say I have a knack for helping people," she replied.

Lucy sighed, and the smug grin on Becky's face widened when she said. "Fine, I'll do it."

Becky clapped her hands together. "This will be fun," she murmured, took out a pen and scribbled her contact details on the paper. "I will expect a call from you."

Lucy watched her walk away after that and rubbed her forehead. "Did you just agree to work an event for free?" Hannah asked, stepping out of the bakery. "I heard the entire conversation," she added when Lucy raised her brows. Hannah pulled out a chair and sat. "You let her bait you."

"She offered excellent prospects," Lucy replied. "More clients... corporate and wealthy clients if I work on this, and the best part is I get to meet them in person. Isn't that great?" she asked, as if in doubt of her decision. She had heard rumors about the Andersons and their need for perfection. There was constant gossip surrounding them, revolving around Becky Anderson's short temper, and the need to stay in control. She wondered if working for the woman was the right choice.

If their alliance didn't turn out as planned, she would offer compensation, right? She rubbed her jaw again and looked at Hannah. "You think it's a good deal? Considering you know all about Becky Anderson through the gossips."

"It's a great deal. Working for Mrs. Anderson shouldn't be

that hard," Hannah replied. "But you don't sound so sure... do you think you made a wrong decision?"

"I don't know." They both fell silent, and Lucy added. "I have a weird gut feeling about it though, and I have to admit, she's quite intimidating," she said as an image of Becky's cool smile flashed in her head.

"I think it will be huge," Hannah exclaimed, and the excitement in her eyes brought a smile to Lucy's face. She pushed down the tingle that had formed in the pit of her stomach and blamed it on over-analysis.

Lucy grinned and handed over the paper she held to Hannah. "Here's a list of the treats needed," she said. "We will start work immediately."

Hannah walked back into the bakery after their brief conversation, and Lucy relaxed in her chair and sighed. This was a new prospect for her, and it could lead to another expansion in her business. "You've come a long way, Lucy," she murmured and exhaled again as she raised her head and shut her eyes, mentally congratulating herself on her accomplishments.

*But why did it feel like there was another wave of unrest coming and something was about to go wrong?*

## 2

*L*ucy hummed to the soft music in the background and sipped from her glass of cranberry juice. She looked around the hall, satisfied at the brilliant smiles on the faces of the guests as they enjoyed her treats. She turned to Becky as she walked across the room to where Lucy stood, and she smiled.

"Lucy," Becky began after she placed a soft peck on Lucy's cheeks. "Every guest in attendance loves your treats. It's all they've talked about since the evening began."

"Thanks," Lucy replied.

"I guess people open their pockets when they have wonderful treats to feast on." Becky laughed and sipped from her glass, her eyes twinkling. An old couple walked towards them, and Becky leaned in and whispered. "Here comes Mr. and Mrs. Wilson."

The couple reached where they stood, and Becky lifted her chin. Lucy watched in amusement as she greeted them. Becky had a stylish way with words. Her rich southern accent made her sound different from the locals, and she played it to her advantage when she spoke in her low, silky tone.

"I'd like to introduce you to the mind behind the wonderful treats," Becky said, and touched Lucy on her shoulder. Lucy smiled.

"Nice to meet you, Lucy," Mrs. Wilson said as she shook her hand.

"Likewise."

"I'll leave you all to get acquainted," Becky chirped in with a laugh before walking away. Lucy fixed her attention on the couple, and Mr. Wilson smiled at her.

"Wonderful evening," he said. "I enjoyed the cupcakes best," he added, and his wife slapped his arm playfully.

"You've had way too many of those tonight, Lucas," she chided. "You're not having any from the next serving."

"Fine," he laughed. "I'll take the kale chips next or maybe I'll try some of those truffles."

Lucy joined in the rumble of light laughter, and Mr. Wilson continued. "I love the cupcakes because of the sprinkles, dear. They twinkle, just like the stars in the sky."

"Thank you," Lucy replied, and turned to Mrs. Wilson. "Did you enjoy the treats, too?"

"Of course, I did."

"Sarah will turn seventy-five soon, and we would like something with sprinkles for the party," Lucas cut in. He turned to Sarah and gave her a warm smile. He grinned at Sarah, and Lucy saw his eyes gleam, and she could tell they loved each other.

"It's also our fiftieth anniversary. Would you like to cater for the event?"

Lucy was giddy with excitement at what she had just heard and couldn't hide the grin on her face that seemed to stretch from one ear to the other. "I would love to!"

They walked away after Lucy accepted the business card Mr. Wilson handed over, and as she stared at it, she smiled.

*Guess this wasn't such a bad idea after all,* she thought, grinning.

Still staring at the business card in her hand, she picked up a glass of cranberry juice from a waiter's tray. Lucy hadn't expected working with Becky to turn out easy, but everything, so far, had worked out just fine. They had agreed on the treats and Becky had no problem with Lucy adding a few items like kale chips, truffles, and caramel-apple tarts.

"It's amazing what you did with the cupcakes," a voice said, pulling her out of her thoughts, and Lucy turned to see Taylor, the town's deputy sheriff. His dark eyes flickered from her face to the cupcake he held.

Lucy had been romantically involved with Taylor before she left Ivy Creek for the big city. Everyone thought they would be together forever. Lucy thought so too, and she knew Taylor felt the same. But she chose to pursue her dreams to have a career in the big city and that had spelt the end of their relationship. Ever since she had gotten back in town, Taylor had made it known implicitly and explicitly that she wasn't welcome.

"You're turning into a celebrity," he said when they both turned to see Becky smile and wave at her from a distance.

"I wasn't expecting to see you here," she replied, licking her suddenly dry lips. She didn't always know what reaction to expect whenever she saw him, considering their shared history. Her relationship with Taylor lasted a while, so she was used to reading his facial expressions.

"I got an invitation as a member of the town council committee," he replied and looked around the hall. "The party is well organized."

Lucy accepted the compliment and assessed him briefly.

He wore a jet-black suit, and clean black shoes. The look made him fit into the business world perfectly. *He cleans up nicely for a guy who loves jeans and plain baggy t-shirts,* she thought.

"Well, I hope you enjoy the rest of your evening," she said and he smiled.

"I will."

Lucy excused herself and joined Becky, who stood beside her husband, sharing a conversation. She saw their lips move as they talked, and when she got to them, she greeted Mr. Anderson with a smile and made eye contact with Becky.

"You've put together a lovely event," Becky complimented. "It's been a wonderful evening."

"We owe you our gratitude, Lucy," he replied. "Without the treats, we wouldn't get half the response we've gotten from the guests. You've impressed them, and also opened their wallets."

Lucy laughed at his remark and withdrew her hand from his. "I will definitely recommend you to my clients who are glad to pay for quality services like yours. *James Anderson* represents most of the wealthy members of the town, and I will always recommend you."

"Thank you, sir," she replied, and he shook his head.

"Please, call me Roland," he corrected. "I'd love to be on a first name basis."

He gave Becky a brief kiss on the lips before he walked away, and Becky turned to her. "So, was working with me a success?"

"It was," she admitted, wondering why everyone in town thought Becky was a socially distant, rude woman. Lucy found her intimidating at first, but when they conversed more, she realized there was nothing to Becky's personality besides outstanding self-esteem.

"You've only just begun," she added and walked away.

Lucy spent the rest of the evening socializing amongst the guests, and by the end of the event, all she could think of was getting home and taking off the black stilettos she had to wear all evening to complement her red, backless evening dress.

Hannah joined her in the parking lot when it was time to go, and she helped her lift the bag she held into the back seat of the car.

"Have fun?" Hannah asked as she took off the cap she wore over her short blonde hair. Hannah had worked with the catering team Becky had hired to make sure they served the treats and presented drinks to the guests properly.

"I met a few prestigious guests and guess what?" Lucy replied. She took out the business card Mr. Wilson gave her. "I got a new job offer."

Hannah squealed, and laughing, they both got into Lucy's car. She explained the details of the birthday deal to Hannah as they drove down the road and headed for Hannah's house downtown.

Still overwhelmed with joy, Lucy hummed a nursery rhyme to herself as she drove back to her apartment after dropping Hannah off. When she walked up the stairs and entered her room, Gigi, her white Persian cat, greeted her with a loud purr.

"Hey, Gigi," she greeted. Lucy squatted and ruffled Gigi's fur, smiling as Gigi rubbed her body around her legs. "Miss me?" she asked as she sat on the floor, unbuckled her shoes, and kicked them off.

Lucy sighed and massaged the heels of each foot gently, and relaxed against the wall. "I had a great night," she continued as Gigi watched her with wide eyes, her tail straight and upright. Lucy stroked Gigi again and closed her eyes.

*I shouldn't have worried so much,* she thought as she settled in bed thirty minutes later.

The evening had turned out great. She had prospective new clients and a growing reputation in town. Everything was perfect, and she had a lot of work to look forward to this summer. *What could possibly go wrong at this point?*

## 3

*T*he next day, Lucy kept herself busy with preparing a new batch of pastries for sale.

Humming to the music playing from her ear pods, Lucy spun around in the kitchen and stepped to the beat. She didn't hear Hannah come into the kitchen, but when Hannah reached the table where Lucy stood, watching the dough in the industrial mixer, she took off the ear pods.

"I set everything else for the pecan pie in the refrigerator," Hannah announced, wiping her flour covered hands on a napkin she picked from the table. "Do you need anything else before I go home for the evening?"

Lucy paused and thought about the question for a second before replying. "No, I've got everything else covered."

Hannah pulled out a chair and sat while Lucy tasted the already mixed dough. She had to deliver bread to the grocery store tomorrow, and also cupcakes to a parent who ordered treats for her child's school bake sale.

"Is the bake sale order set?" Hannah asked. "I could help you deliver them tonight before heading home," she offered.

Hannah was always of great help at the main bakery, and

without her, Lucy was certain she would overwork herself. She definitely couldn't handle the bakery and her concession store on her own. "You deserve a raise," she replied, and Hannah chuckled.

"Does that mean I will get one soon?"

"Of course." Lucy smiled as she wrapped the dough in a cling film and placed it in her refrigerator. She had to wait forty-five minutes before placing it in the oven, and she could use those minutes to sort out the cupcake order for the bake sale.

"I should call the Wilsons this weekend to follow up and get more details about the birthday," Lucy said as they wrapped each cupcake in a fancy material.

"That's a brilliant idea," Hannah replied. "The Wilsons own more than half the grocery stores in Ivy Creek, and if this deal goes well, you might become a major supplier of their pastries."

Lucy looked forward to the possibility of being their major supplier. She could work towards opening another bakery soon if things continued running smoothly, and her blog - Lucy's Food Blog - still brought more publicity to her business.

"Working that event with Becky has turned out to be a blessing," she commented. When they finished wrapping the cakes, Lucy's phone rang, and she stepped out of the kitchen to take the call.

"Aunt Tricia," she said when she heard her aunt's smooth laugh on the other end. "It's been a while."

"I've been great, dear... how are you?" she replied, and Lucy smiled.

The last time she spoke with her aunt, Tricia had mentioned her decision to move back to Ivy Creek, and Lucy had helped her check out some houses her real estate agent had suggested. Two of them were a stone's throw from her parents' house on Third Avenue, and the last one was close to the town's high school.

Whichever choice Tricia made, she would be a thirty minutes' drive away from the bakery, and Lucy preferred that. "I've been great, Aunty. A lot has happened here, and guess what... I got to work for the rich and famous owner of *James Anderson*," she said, unable to hold the news from her aunt. Her voice oozed with conviction as she added. "I think that's just the beginning of my expansion, and soon Sweet Delights will be all over the country."

Tricia laughed. "You have big dreams, dear," she replied, and cleared her throat.

"How's the relocation plans coming along? I should have called sooner, but the past week has been hectic on my end," Lucy explained, and turned around when Hannah stepped into the dining area.

"I turned down the heat of the oven," Hannah whispered, and walked back into the kitchen.

The warm, slightly sweet aroma of the bread, filled the air and it reminded Lucy of her childhood before the bakery started running. Her mother's passion was always baking, and Sweet Delights was her parents' dream. They started it, but never got to see it expand beyond that single shop before they passed away. Lucy was fulfilling those dreams with each sale and deal she made.

Lucy shifted her attention back to her aunt on the other end, who was explaining the bits of her relocation plans.

"So, you'll make the last move by the end of the week?" Lucy asked when Tricia finished her explanations.

"Yes... I never thought I would move back to Ivy Creek, but here I am," she replied, and laughed again. "I will talk to you later, Lucy. Have to take another call."

"Bye," Lucy said, and the phone beeped as the call ended. With a sigh, she joined Hannah in the kitchen. "That was

Tricia," she said, and Hannah pulled open the top shelf and took out a bowl. She placed it on the table, took out a pack of whipped cream from the refrigerator, and measured out the amount needed.

They had to prepare coconut flavored whipped toppings for the cupcakes they'd be selling the next day. Lucy loved to prepare everything beforehand to make the day less stressful.

As Hannah whipped the cream, she asked. "When is she making the final move?"

"By the weekend. I'm glad she's moving back to town… having her around is helpful."

Lucy enjoyed having Tricia around because she was the only extended family she had left. Tricia was her mother's elder sister, and her father had no siblings. Later that evening, Lucy was happy to send Hannah off with the packed cupcakes which she'd be delivering to their customer. She stayed a few more hours in the bakery before turning in for the day.

———

THE NEXT DAY was unlike any Lucy had experienced in her bakery's short existence. It was super busy. Customers strolled in and out of the bakery, and orders kept coming in for delivery. John, the driver Lucy hired for home deliveries, came into the store while Lucy was closing a client's birthday cake order, and she beamed at him.

"Here's a tip," she said and handed over a ten-dollar bill to him. John smiled and tucked the note into his wallet before taking the paper bag of orders. "Thanks, John."

"Anytime," he replied, and strolled out of the bakery. Lucy walked around the counter and smiled when another customer walked in.

"Welcome to Sweet Delights. What would you like?"

"Three cupcakes with sprinkles to go please," the girl replied, and stuck out a ten-dollar bill.

"That will be seven dollars, and thirty-five cents," Lucy said.

Lucy attended to a few more customers until Hannah returned from the restroom and took over. Lucy went into the kitchen to prepare the bread delivery she had for the day.

She supplied three grocery stores in town with pastries twice a week, as well as two families who ordered special pastries like gluten-free and vegan bread. When she finished arranging the bread inside her delivery basket, she glanced at her watch.

"Keisha will be here any minute," she murmured and took off the apron she wore. Lucy stepped out of the kitchen and as she got into the sitting area, the door opened and Keisha, the sales assistant from the grocery store down the high street, walked in.

"Hey, Keisha," Hannah greeted. Keisha placed her hands on the counter and exhaled. Lucy noticed she looked flushed, and her eyes were wide as she panted.

"Are you alright?" she asked, and Keisha struggled to catch her breath. "You look flushed."

Keisha placed her hands on her cheeks and swallowed. "I'm also hot," she replied and shuddered.

Lucy watched Keisha shut her eyes tight for a moment, and then she reopened them as she wiped some beads of sweat that her were forming on her forehead.

Hannah asked, "Did something happen?"

"You both didn't hear?" Keisha replied, her wide hollow eyes darting across Lucy's and Hannah's. "The entire town has heard about it."

Lucy stiffened, and color drained from her cheeks as Keisha added. "Mr. Wilson died last night, and his wife is still unconscious."

---

## 4

*K*eisha's announcement left Lucy speechless. She blinked multiple times as she tried to process what she had just heard.

"I heard they got ill from food poisoning. Mr. Wilson is dead, but his wife is still unconscious," Keisha said.

"When... when did they get hospitalized?" Lucy stammered. She exhaled, trying to keep calm, but her insides tightened and the horror of Keisha's news made her heart ache.

"After the Andersons' party," Keisha replied, and Lucy took two steps backward. She collided with the counter behind her, and Hannah reached a hand out to steady her. *The night of the party?*

Shivering, Lucy wrapped her arms around her sides and turned away, hurrying into the kitchen. Minutes later, Hannah joined her. "Keisha just left with the bread supplies," Hannah said, and Lucy turned to her.

Lucy murmured, "I can't believe I might be linked to another murder in town."

"Why would you say that, Lucy?" Hannah replied. "A lot

of guests had your treats that night. You don't see them dying in hospitals, do you?"

"I know that, but..."

"Let's relax, Lucy," Hannah advised. "The cops will sort this out."

Lucy hoped that was the case, and she swallowed, trying to fight the gut-wrenching feeling of doom closing in on her. Keisha's words replayed in her head, *Speculations are they got ill from food poisoning.* An image of Mr. and Mrs. Wilson's smiles flashed in her head, and she clenched her fists as a wave of nausea hit her.

Lucy rushed to the sink, turned on the faucet, and splashed the cold water on her face, hoping it could jar her out of this bad dream. She could feel tears forming in her eyes, so she splashed the water again, and placed her hands on the edge of the sink, leaning in towards it.

"We have a customer," Hannah said, but Lucy didn't turn back.

*What do I do? Why is this happening again? Who could have done this?*

Her mind reeled with questions, and she reached for her phone and dialed Tricia's number. Her aunt picked up on the second ring, and her smooth voice helped Lucy's nerves relax. The first time she was involved in a murder investigation, her aunt's support helped get her through it.

"Aunt Tricia," she began in a shaky voice.

"Are you alright, dear?" Tricia replied in a hushed tone.

"I'm in trouble again," she replied and shut her eyes tight. The dull throb in her head spread, and when she opened her eyes again, tears slipped down her cheeks. "There's another murder investigation in Ivy Creek."

Lucy spent the next ten minutes on the phone with her aunt, explaining the events of the night and the news of Mr. Wilson's death. She ended the call when Tricia promised to come into town sooner than planned, and Hannah rushed into the kitchen.

"Lucy, Taylor's here," she whispered. Lucy wiped her cheeks, tucked her phone into the back pocket of her jeans, and exhaled to steady herself. She headed out to the dining area, and when Taylor turned to her, she saw the question in his eyes, and she spoke before he said anything.

"I don't know how this happened."

"I can't believe there's another murder, and somehow it involves you," he replied, shaking his head and tapping his fingers on the counter.

A few months ago, Lucy had been involved in a murder investigation when the owner of a rival bakery had died. His corpse was found in Lucy's backyard and she had been identified as a prime suspect. Taylor had been in charge of the investigation and because of the history between them, he had done nothing to allay her fears that she would be found guilty. Thankfully, the real killer was eventually found but it seemed she was still in Taylor's bad books.

"Is it a murder investigation?" she stammered.

Taylor hesitated before replying. "Nothing is certain for now. We're trying to rule out foul play, and that's why I am here," he paused, and looked around the dining area. "I'm here to collect samples of the treats served that night."

"My treats can't possibly be the cause," Lucy defended. "You know that. You had them too and you're not dead."

"Lucy..." he called, his voice trailing off. "Please, just go along with this investigation. Let's make this easier on both of us this time, and I suggest you don't leave town while the investigation is ongoing as that puts you in a difficult position."

She lowered her head for a second. "I think I have some cupcakes and kale chips left," she replied, and led him into the kitchen. Taylor collected the treat samples in an evidence bag, and Lucy walked him to the front of the bakery before asking.

"Any news about Mrs. Wilson's condition?" Taylor rubbed the back of his neck. "Will she be alright?"

"Mrs. Wilson died a few hours ago."

She staggered backwards, her mouth suddenly going dry. Lucy clutched her chest and watched as he walked to his truck parked on the other side of the road. The knots in her stomach tightened, and she lifted her shaky hands to her cheeks.

Her chest was so tight, she couldn't breathe properly, and the urge to scream built up with each second. *Would screaming help?* She wondered. *Would it take away some of this tightness in my chest?*

Hours ago, she was certain her fate had changed, and her business was on the verge of expanding, and now... everything was spiraling downhill so fast, it gave her no time to prepare for the impact of a crash.

Shoulders dropping low, Lucy walked back into the bakery, and turned the door sign to *Closed*. She stared at the *closed* sign and wondered if it was a sign. A sign that it was time to pack in and return to the big city where she previously had a life.

## 5

_L_ucy flipped over to her left side on her bed and dragged the sheets over her body. She willed her mind to stop spinning, so she could get a decent amount of sleep, but nothing she did brought relief to her racing heart.

It was barely dawn, and this made it the fourth day since news about the Wilsons' death broke. Over the past few days, Lucy had listened as rumors about their death, spread throughout the entire town.

The previous night, a client of hers had called to cancel her order for a birthday party. She gave the excuse of not hosting a large party anymore, so homemade desserts would suffice. But Lucy could tell it was a lie because the woman stuttered a lot as she framed her sentences.

Her aunt promised to come in before the weekend, and she desperately needed the support of family if she was going to get through this stage.

With a sigh, she threw the covers off her body and slipped out of bed, heading to the bathroom for a quick, cold shower to calm her nerves. Lucy spread her rose-scented wash over her skin, and inhaled the blends of floral scents, hoping it would help ease her insides.

When she finished in the shower, she strolled to the kitchen downstairs to fix a quick cup of hot cocoa. Lucy weighed her options. She could stay in town, and allow the investigation to run its course, or she could drop everything now and leave town. The last time a murder investigation involved her, business had flopped, and she had struggled together with Hannah and her aunt Tricia to keep the bakery afloat.

She had been so optimistic about the future of her business a few days back, but now she couldn't think of one reason to keep the business running. Lucy finished her cocoa, stood up from her seat, and opened the bakery. Hannah was due to arrive at 8 a.m., but Lucy always opened before she arrived. She cleaned the front glass, turned the outside sign to 'Now Open', and walked into the kitchen to note the pastries they had in stock.

"I have made no sales in the past two days," she muttered, chewing on her lower lip as she opened the refrigerator and took out a bowl of sliced fruits. At this rate, she would run at a loss soon. "What's the point of all of this, anyway?"

With her stomach rumbling, Lucy took out her phone to call her aunt. She needed some reassurance as nothing she did seemed to stop her heart from thudding louder with each passing second.

She heard a soft knock, and the slow creak of the front door caught her attention. She dropped her phone on the table and rushed to the dining area.

"Aunt Tricia," she exclaimed as Tricia stepped into the bakery. A black duffel bag hung loosely on one shoulder, and she held her car keys in the other. Lucy was in her arms in a split second. She exhaled and stepped back after a second.

"You look like you've lost some weight," Tricia

commented as Lucy took her bag. "Have you been over-thinking?"

The rumbles in the pit of her stomach slowly subsided, and she rubbed the back of her neck as she dropped the bag in a corner of the kitchen. "I can't help it, Aunt Tricia. It's like I'm deep in quicksand, and things might keep going downhill from this point."

"Don't be quick to assume things, honey. I know life isn't fair but giving up so easily isn't your style."

"I hate this," Lucy whispered. "Hate that I'm in this position again… helpless again. Taylor dropped by here a few days back. He took some cupcakes as samples for testing."

"They think your treats caused their death?" Tricia asked. "You have no motive to want the Wilsons dead," she pointed out.

Lucy nodded, bit her lower lip, and dropped into a chair. She crossed her hands on the table. "They died after the party hosted by the Andersons. I was with them for a while during the party, and they both looked healthy and so in love. The doctors suspect food poisoning, and the last place they were seen alive and well was at the party."

Tricia tapped a finger on the table continuously, and she tilted her head. "I lived in Ivy Creek the first thirty-five years of my life, and I know what it's like around here when there's something newsworthy, but the gossip mongers can't feast on one piece of news for too long and soon latch on to something else."

Lucy remembered Aunt Tricia moved out when her husband got a job in Denver. They had rented a condo by the lake in a nearby town called Castle Pines. Lucy had visited one summer with her parents and Tricia had shown them the mountainous path of the Colorado leading to the Denver River. The memory was special to her as Tricia had tucked her in that night and told her a story about a one-eyed monster who lived in the mountains.

"What happens to my business while I wait for this to blow over? Just like the last time, no one comes by here anymore, and it's only just the first week."

Tricia placed her hand over Lucy's and squeezed. "Don't beat yourself up. I believe the truth will eventually come out. In the meantime, how about we distract ourselves with a trip to the convenience store? I need some personal items."

"Hannah should be here any minute," Lucy replied, and rose from her chair. She glanced at her watch and added. "We can leave for the store once she shows up."

Lucy carried her aunt's bag to the extra bedroom upstairs and Gigi followed her into the room, flicking her tail. Tricia came into the bedroom and took off the shawl wrapped around her neck.

"Hi, Gigi," Tricia greeted, and squatted to stroke Gigi's fur. Gigi gave a high-pitched meow. "I will take a brief nap, and join you downstairs soon," she said and smiled at Lucy. "Try to worry less dear."

"I will."

Lucy walked out of the bedroom with Gigi, shutting the door gently behind her. "Come on, let's fix you breakfast," she whispered and scooped Gigi into her arms.

Hannah arrived while she was waiting for the homemade salmon recipe to cool off, and she greeted Lucy with an enthusiastic voice. She stroked Gigi's fur and walked over to the sink to wash her hands. "I see Tricia's sedan parked behind yours in the corner. When did she get here?"

"Not so long ago. She's resting upstairs right now."

"It's good to have her around," Hannah replied. "You need to stop worrying so much about everything. I'm sure it will blow over soon, and now that Tricia is here, you can distract yourself a little."

Lucy remained quiet, and Hannah checked the stock. "Did we get any orders this morning?"

"No," Lucy replied, and stopped stirring the kibble. "Mrs. De Luca called to cancel the order for her son's birthday next weekend. She claims they won't be having a large scale party anymore."

Hannah wiped her hands on a dry napkin. "Mrs. De Luca never entertains guests on a small scale. That's obviously a lie."

Lucy squeezed her eyes shut for a second. "I know it is," she replied, and swallowed as she reopened them. Hannah pulled out their inventory notepad from the mini drawer on the left of the kitchen and pulled out a chair at the rectangular table to seat. "There's nothing we can do besides wait for the cops to clear this up and find the killer."

"Did you hear from Taylor?" Hannah asked.

"No," she replied in a tiny voice. "But I hope to hear something soon."

Gigi finished her meal, and Lucy cleaned the plate before heading back to her room. When she returned to the bakery minutes later, Tricia was sitting with Hannah on the patio, enjoying a glass of lemonade.

Lucy stepped onto the patio and shut the door behind her. She took a seat at the table and picked a crepe from Hannah's plate. "Ready for a drive to the store?" Lucy asked.

Tricia nodded her reply and emptied her glass. "I was just telling Hannah of my theory after thinking about the details you told me."

Lucy arched a questioning brow in Hannah's direction. "What theory?"

"The Wilsons are a close-knit family, and many people in Ivy Creek envied the relationship they had," Hannah replied. "It seems preposterous that anyone would hate or want them dead… They had no enemies anyone was aware of."

"Which brings my theory to life," Tricia said. "What if the killer is a close relative? Someone whom no one would suspect?"

"What are you thinking?" Lucy asked, her face scrunched up. Whatever Tricia's theory was, it could prove useful. Everyone was a suspect until proven innocent, and if Lucy didn't kill them, then their killer was out there. A chill coiled up Lucy's spine from the thought of someone ending two innocent lives, and her stomach rumbled.

"The Wilsons had two sons. I met them once while I lived here, and again last year," Tricia replied. "If we want to dig into close relatives, then their sons come first."

"They each run a subsidiary of their parents' grocery store business," Hannah said. "You think one of them is the killer? Isn't that a wild assumption?"

"She's not saying one of them is the killer," Lucy replied before Tricia could speak. "She's saying we have a premise to dig up what we can."

Tricia's smile turned upward. "It's a good thing we planned a trip to the convenience store," she mumbled, and rose from her seat. "Let's see what we can find out."

## 6

*A* sheen of sweat broke out on Lucy's forehead as they walked into the Wilsons' convenience store downtown twenty minutes later.

She walked over to the counter behind her aunt, and Lucy's gaze wandered around, sizing up the store's symmetrical arrangements. She picked up the fruity smell, and the clean atmosphere made the place relaxing.

Although the store was empty, the man at the counter kept busy. He kept his focus on the screen before him, his fingers punching his keyboard as if he had a personal vendetta against it. Tricia leaned towards Lucy as they neared the counter. "That's Bruce... he's their first son. I recognize him because we passed by each other a few times last year when I was in town. He was with his father one of those times."

Lucy assessed his slight frame, noting the crease lines on his forehead as he focused on what he was doing. He stopped typing, rubbed the stubble on his jaw, and continued.

"Mr. Wilson," Tricia called, gaining his attention, and his jaw dropped when he looked in their direction.

His gaze landed on hers, and Lucy nearly cowered behind her aunt when his brown eyes bulged out.

"I'm Tricia King," her aunt added.

"Lucy Hale," she said after Tricia.

"I know who you are," Bruce replied, and took his hands off the keyboard. He slipped them into his pockets and leaned away from the counter. "The town keeps talking about you."

"I'm here to relay my condolences about your parents," Lucy replied. She placed her hand over her chest gently. "You should know I had nothing to do with it like the rumors say and accept my sincerest condolences."

"I don't pay attention to the rumors," he replied in an edgy tone. "People lose sight of what's important when they focus on what everyone thinks. Whatever information I need about my parents' death, I will get from the cops."

Lucy nodded and shifted her weight from one foot to the other. Bruce Wilson turned away from her, and she released an exasperated sigh. His reaction was far different from what she had imagined. She had expected him to meet her with anger.

"Still, it must be hard for you," Tricia added. "Losing your parents in such a way… it's not something I would wish on anyone. We are truly sorry for your loss."

He nodded, his tight expression easing a little. "Thank you," he replied. "I've had many condolences come in since they passed away, and yours seems more genuine than curious. I appreciate that…" His words trailed off as the door swung open, and a man walked in, holding three large boxes.

Lucy and Tricia exchanged curious looks as Bruce ordered the man to place the boxes in the back and handed over the receipts.

"They are new stock. I'm doing a general restock of this store and our branch on sixth avenue," he said when he turned back to them. "It's Thanksgiving soon, and a lot of families have guests for Thanksgiving. It's a good business time for the store, and it would help with our expansion next year."

"Expansion?" Lucy asked. Would anyone who just lost their loved ones a few days ago be thinking of expanding a business? Lucy tried to hide her suspicion with a follow-up question.

"Wouldn't those plans take a back burner considering the ongoing investigations and funeral preparations?"

Bruce shrugged. "My parents weren't religious. They would have wanted to be cremated without a funeral, and we've pushed back plans of expansion for long enough. It's now or never," he replied with a wave of his hand.

"It's good to see you making steady plans," Tricia chirped in. She took Lucy's hand in hers and squeezed. "Take care," she added, and led Lucy out of the store.

Outside, Tricia released Lucy, and Lucy combed her fingers through her hair. "Seems to me like Bruce Wilson has everything figured out," she commented, and glanced back at the store as they walked to Tricia's car in the parking space.

Tricia turned on the engine when they got in and sped down the road. She tapped her finger on the steering wheel as she drove. "Don't you think he's suspicious?"

"It just seemed to me like he wasn't grieving at all. Either that, or he is excellent at masking it or shoving it away."

"He was quick to dismiss the rumors surrounding his parents' death and his talk of expansion made him seem like he didn't care about his parents' death."

"Let's drop by his brother's store and see what we can find."

———

THE LOCATION of Wayne's store was a mile away from Bruce's, and Lucy had a hunch that they didn't see eye to eye on the expansion because when they arrived at the store Wayne was closing up.

Lucy glanced at her watch, wondering why he would close the store so early in the day. "Wayne Wilson," she called, and he turned around.

Wayne was a foot taller than his brother, and his height, coupled with the broad expanse of his shoulders, made him look older than Bruce.

He adjusted the bag on his shoulder and waited till they reached him. "Lucy Hale?" he called in a shaky voice, and a dull ache formed in the pit of her stomach. *Maybe Wayne Wilson would treat her with anger and not indifference like his brother*, she thought.

"Yes," she replied.

He frowned, and Lucy began in carefully spaced words. "I'm here to relay my sincerest condolences for your parents' deaths. I met them once, and they were really friendly people."

Wayne's head bobbed nervously, and he licked his lips. "They were," he replied, his voice cracking.

"I'm truly sorry about the news," Tricia added. "It must be so hard on you, having to work on funeral arrangements, and the store expansion."

Wayne stared at the ground, and when he raised them, his eyes were watery. "I admit I've had it rough, but I'm holding it together. When it gets too hard, I take time out to cool off. I've never imagined a world without my parents in it."

His words reminded Lucy of the ache in her heart when she received the news of her parents' death some months ago. She remembered being confused at first, before her aunt's words sank in fully, and the tears that came after did nothing to reduce the gut-wrenching pain.

"It gets easier with time," she assured him, and looked around the surroundings of the store to the black model T Ford parked in the tall grass beside the store.

Wayne jiggled the keys in his hands as Tricia asked, "Were you heading out?"

"Yes," he replied. "I have an appointment, and I really didn't feel like opening until the funeral passed, but Bruce insisted. He has always had more zeal for the business, and my parents thought he made a better successor because I ran things differently. But even though I don't share his focus and zeal, I have compassion and I think the key to running a successful business is making your customers comfortable, and happy. I'd rather close up than allow my poor state of mind to affect the business."

"You do what you have to do to feel better," Tricia sympathized, and a sigh escaped his lips.

"Thanks for your visit, Miss Hale. It means a lot that you both dropped by."

"Please, it's Lucy," she replied and gave him a warm smile.

Wayne walked away from them, and they watched as he entered the Ford, kick started the engine, and disappeared down the rutted road.

"Well, that sure looked like grieving," Tricia said as they walked back to her car. "He seems more affected by his parents' death than Bruce."

Lucy shook her head. "He showed compassion... it's human to show your pain," she replied and stared at the road as Tricia swerved the sedan down the single lane. "I think Bruce is ambitious."

"That makes him dangerous," Tricia replied. "A person with ambition always craves more, and you never know the lengths they'd take to achieve their ambition. But then again, Wayne wasn't as good at business as his brother, and his parents made it clear Bruce was a better successor. He could have just the same ambition as his brother."

Lucy agreed with her. Wayne was just as suspicious as his brother because he also had a motive. If his parents undermined him, then at some point he would seek to disprove this, and that made him as dangerous as Bruce.

"We might be on to something here," Tricia said, and stole a glance at her. "I have a feeling there's more to Bruce Wilson."

"Likewise, Wayne," Lucy replied, replaying the emotional scene with him earlier. She couldn't trust either of them because the chances that they both put on an act were high.

## 7

*L*ucy noticed Hannah was sitting outside the bakery with a glum look on her face as they got out of the car. She walked over to her and dropped into a chair. "Any customers?" she asked, hoping some news would brighten her mood.

"None," Hannah replied, and rubbed the back of her neck. "I've been sitting out here all day, and not even one person dropped by."

Lucy lowered her head into her hands. She rubbed her temples slowly, hoping it would dull the slow ache she had there all day, and ease some of her tension.

A minute of silence passed between the three women before she spoke. "I had a bad feeling about working with Becky Anderson," she murmured. "Guess I should have listened to my gut!"

"You can't blame yourself for any of this," Hannah said. "Becky presented a good business offer, and you took it."

"I'm in this mess because I agreed to make treats for her party."

"Were you compensated for the work done?" Tricia asked.

"You put in a lot of effort and now have more troubles because of the murder."

"I did the work for free," Lucy replied, and Tricia's jaw dropped. Lucy shook her head and unwrapped the shawl around her neck.

"You knew better, Lucy," Tricia chided. "You're a talented businesswoman. I've watched you grow this place over the past few months. How did you let some uppity woman talk you into working for free? You should have gotten something for your troubles."

Lucy groaned and closed her eyes for a second. *I shouldn't have worked at this party.... I'm in this mess because of Becky Anderson's proposal.*

"Have you heard from her since the beginning of all of this? Has she contacted you to say anything? Maybe offer to defend you?" Tricia asked.

"She hasn't," Hannah replied for Lucy, and a heavy sigh escaped Lucy's lips. An engine roared from across the road, and Lucy straightened her spine. The car slowed by the side of the bakery and stopped.

"That's Becky," Hannah announced once the driver stepped out of the car.

Tricia and Hannah walked into the bakery, leaving Lucy to confront Becky alone. Lucy remained in her seat as Becky marched towards her patio. She wore a neatly pressed white chiffon blouse tucked into green pants, and her hair tied into a sleek ponytail.

"I should tread carefully when hiring for an event next time," Becky began, with no niceties. "What exactly did you do? How did you make such a mess of the opportunity I handed over to you by causing a ruckus and a murder investigation?"

"I don't know what you mean, but if it's about the Wilsons, then you've come to the wrong place. I am just as confused as you are or anyone else in this town."

"This entire episode has damaged my brand, and it's all your fault, Lucy Hale. You served those treats at the party. You should be responsible."

"Are you accusing me of killing the Wilsons?" Lucy asked, raising her voice a notch. Her eyes widened in disbelief, and she blinked rapidly. "What reason would I have to kill them? I never met them before your party."

"You did this... you should be responsible... perhaps you made a mistake with the recipe or something? Maybe they were allergic to something in your cupcakes. I don't know, but it was something they ate from your treats. That's on you!"

"No, it's not," Lucy defended. Her cheeks burned with the ferocity of her growing anger, and she could barely contain the tremble in her voice as she jabbed a finger at Becky. "You don't get to drive here in your expensive suit and car and accuse me of killing people. It was your party... your association, and if someone poisoned the Wilsons, then it would be someone on your list of guest. Other guests had my treats. How many of them did you see dropping dead from poisoning?"

The door opened, and Tricia stepped out of the bakery. Lucy shoved her fingers through her hair when her aunt placed a hand on her arm to calm her.

"I won't let you blame me for any of this," Lucy added, and turned away from Becky.

She struggled to regain composure. Her nerves were spiraling from her recent outburst, and from the ashen look on Becky's face, she could tell she had surprised her, too. Lucy prided herself on having a tight control over her emotions. She never let them get the best of her, but everything about this situation was testing her resilience.

Becky dropped into a chair. Her purse landed by her feet, and she rubbed her forehead.

"I understand how difficult it is trying to run a business right now because of the ongoing investigation, but throwing accusations around won't change that," Tricia pointed out.

Lucy turned to see the pout on Becky's lips. "I'm sorry," Becky muttered. "Since all of this started, I've had a massive decline in profits and my husband and I are trying hard to get to the root of this. When I heard the Wilsons died, and they suspected it was food poisoning that killed them, I dropped by here. I don't think your treats caused their death... I had some of your cupcakes and they were amazing. I guess I let my emotions get the best of me."

"I'm sorry, too," Lucy replied.

A relieved look washed over Becky's face, and she continued. "I know the cops will sort this out. We just have to give them time to do their job. All my customers withdrew their orders, and the bakery makes no daily sales."

"It's hard," Becky murmured and crossed her legs. "I have Roland's support, and it makes things easier to know I have that one person in my corner rooting for me."

Lucy leaned forward and tapped her finger on the table. *I wish I had that;* she thought. *A person in my corner, rooting for me, backing me up all the way.*

"How are you holding up?" Becky asked.

"I'm hanging in... holding on to a shred of hope it will work out." Lucy replied.

"If you need anything, or any help, please reach out to me. I would be more than glad to help in any way I can," Becky replied with a soft smile. She sprung out of her chair then and turned to Tricia. "I'm sorry I barged in here and caused a scene."

"It's not a problem," Tricia replied with a nod. They watched Becky walk to her car and drive away before Tricia added. "That could have quickly escalated if you didn't control yourself. You should keep Becky Anderson in your corner for the time being. She might be of help someday."

"I'm just so tense… I need to cool off," Lucy replied, and cast Tricia a slight glance.

The creamy scent of buttery cinnamon rolls reached her nose, and her stomach grumbled. She ran a hand over her face, rubbed her nose and inhaled the scent. "Becky's lucky," she whispered, turning to Tricia. "She has someone backing her and helping her through this rough patch. I have no one to lean on besides myself."

"You have me, Lucy," Tricia reminded her, and reached out to touch her hand on the table. "You will always have me."

8

---

 $\mathcal{B}$ usiness worsened over the next three days, and by the weekend, Lucy's clients were not picking up her calls or were canceling their orders. She checked her watch for the tenth time since Hannah arrived an hour ago and let out a heavy sigh when she realized it was almost noon.

Hannah, sitting at a corner of the bakery's dining area, repeatedly tapped her finger on the table, and the noise made Lucy nervous. She shifted in her chair and cast a glance in Hannah's direction.

"Can you stop doing that? It's making me nervous," she said.

Hannah withdrew her hands from the round wooden table and lifted her left shoulder. "I can't help it, I'm sorry."

Lucy stood up and crossed over to where Hannah sat. "I'm just as worried as you are, maybe even worse than you are. I don't know what to do at this point... It feels like I've lost everything over the past two weeks."

"We need to hang in longer. This will pass, and everything

will be back to normal as soon as the cops clear it up," Hannah reassured her, but Lucy's unsettled insides continued to roll. She couldn't bring herself to stop worrying.

She threw herself into an intense round of cleaning, finding new places to clean in the kitchen and dining area when she had finished the first round of cleaning. Hannah had worked on making a new batch of bread and cupcakes for sale, but in small quantities to minimize loss, and her aunt had worked in the backyard.

Lucy was exhausted by the time she finished. She was still unsettled. *If I could just get an update, anything to give me a shred of hope to hang unto.*

"One customer would encourage me to keep at this," Hannah muttered, but Lucy heard her. "Would you like some salad?"

"Sure," Lucy agreed, and Aunt Tricia walked into the bakery holding a round basket of garden tools Lucy's parents had kept on standby.

"I'm exhausted!"

Lucy re-focused on the task at hand, and Tricia returned from the kitchen with a bottle of cold water. She sat beside Lucy, took a long gulp before asking. "Any customers?"

Lucy shook her head and turned around to see Hannah walking towards her.

"Your cell phone," she said. "Found it buzzing on the table in the kitchen."

Lucy took the phone, and did a double take when she saw the caller ID. Every muscle in her body went rigid, and her breath quickened. "It's Taylor," she murmured. The hand holding the phone trembled slightly, and she broke eye contact with Tricia and focused on the phone.

She watched as the phone vibrated in her hand, contemplating if she was ready to receive the ominous news she was sure he was calling to deliver.

Seconds later, her phone stopped ringing and she closed her eyes. A rush of fear flowed through every vein in her body as she contemplated how bad her situation had become. *What is the worst that can happen? I'm innocent in all this, so I have nothing to worry about.*

"Will you call him back?" Tricia asked, and she nodded twice.

She licked her chapped lips and picked her phone up from the table.

"What's up?" she asked when he picked up on the third ring and stilled herself mentally for his next words. "I have heard no updates from you. Did you call because you have news?"

"Yes," he replied.

"Is the sample testing done? Do we know what killed them yet?" she tried to hide the tremor in her voice but she knew it was obvious.

"We have yet to get the results, but the investigation is officially a murder investigation."

Heart sinking in disappointment, Lucy lowered her gaze to her feet. *What else can go wrong?* She thought in despair, and her eyes turned red from the pool of tears welling up in them.

"Regardless of what happens, please remain in town. We will call you in for questioning, and we will leave no stone unturned," he continued in the same straight tone. "I will be in touch."

Her hand slid to her side when the call ended. She couldn't find it in herself to look at the ladies who she knew were expecting some feedback.

"What did he say?" Tricia and Hannah asked at the same time.

Lucy masked her watery eyes with a grin. "They haven't received a report from the testing yet," she replied. "He promised to be in touch."

"Then why do you look so pale?" Tricia asked, a concerned look on her face.

"I'm fine," she replied. "Excuse me," she added, and hurried out of the bakery. Once outside, she rushed to the side of the building, and dropped both hands on her knees as she fell to the ground.

Lucy's breath came out in haggard puffs, and she struggled to keep breathing against the knot in her throat that promised to suffocate her. *There is no getting out of this... What if this is the end, and they can't prove my innocence? What if the Wilsons truly died because of my treats?*

A torrent of questions bombarded her mind and a hot tear slipped out of her eye. There was a possibility someone had sabotaged her treats to hurt the Wilsons. She couldn't rule out anything yet and it wouldn't be the first time someone in this town was setting her up for a fall.

*I have to contact Becky Anderson...*

Becky organized that party. She had the list of guests who were also possible suspects in Lucy's opinion.

Chest still burning, Lucy regained a bit of composure when she wrapped her hands around her shoulder, and gently patted herself, counting the seconds until her breaths slowed. She heard footsteps followed by her aunt calling, and she staggered to her feet.

"Are you alright, dear? You don't look good." Tricia placed a hand on her arm and led her back to the patio.

"I'm fine," Lucy murmured, stopping Tricia with her hand. "I just need a minute to catch my breath... I'm fine." She had to clear all of this and wrap it up before it got any worse.

Later that evening, Lucy contacted Becky via text. They chose a time and place to meet, and she hoped meeting with Becky would answer her questions.

$\mathcal{T}$he sky was clear the next afternoon, and the air carried a light musky scent of pine and sappy cottonwood. Lucy and Becky met at a local cafeteria downtown, not far off from Ivy Creek High, the school Lucy had attended.

She walked into the cafeteria and chose a spot by the left corner where anyone walking into the shop could easily spot her. It would make it easier for Becky to find her once she got there.

The interior of the shop was cute, with well-polished wooden floors and walls covered in thick, silvery-patterned wallpaper. The choice of colors made the place come alive, and she was impressed with the design as she looked around the half-empty shop.

She imagined that supplying cafeterias like this with her pastries could be a great income earner. It would bring both her bakery and the cafeteria more customers, she thought and turned to the man on the other side of the counter.

He wore an apron over his shirt, and he smiled as he

handed over a to-go coffee cup to the girl at the counter, took the dollar bills she handed over and waved her goodbye.

Lucy flushed when he looked in her direction, and she glanced away. She ran a hand over her sleek ponytail and linked her fingers.

"Hi there," a voice said by her side.

Lucy saw the charming smile on the man's face out of the corner of her eye before turning to meet him.

"I'm Richard Lester," he said, and sat on the chair in front of hers.

She blinked and took in his features. He had a left dimple, she noticed, and the auburn brown shade of his hair matched his golden skin.

"Lucy Hale," she said as she cleared her throat that had suddenly gone dry.

"New to town?" he asked. "I noticed you keep looking over the walls and counter."

"Oh, no, no... I'm here to meet someone," she replied.

Lucy immediately noticed his deep brown eyes as his grin widened. She looked away first when they lingered.

"May I offer something to calm you? You seem rattled, and chamomile tea never goes wrong for soothing nerves," he offered.

"Thank you, but I'm fine. My friend should be here any minute."

"Come on... I insist. It's on the house, I would appreciate if you accepted the gesture."

Lucy looked at him again, and he clasped his hands in a plea gesture. "Alright," she said.

Richard disappeared into the kitchen behind the counter and returned minutes later with a mug on a saucer. Lucy accepted the mug with a warm smile and lifted it to her lips. The underlying refreshing scent of daisies hit her nostrils as she took a sip.

She tasted honey and licked her lip as she lowered the mug to the table. She noticed him watching her, his hooded lids trailing over her face, and Lucy's cheeks turned red.

He leaned forward and laced his fingers on the table. "Soothing, right?" he asked.

Lucy's head bobbed twice, and she sipped from the mug again, wondering if she should suggest a partnership between them. "It's lovely."

"Mind sharing what's bothering you?" he asked.

"It's just business problems," she replied, carefully pacing her words.

"We all have a few of those," Richard replied. "I've had many of those... from renovation problems to lack of customers."

"Really?" Lucy asked and scanned the shop. It seemed like the one thing he didn't lack here was customers. Although the shop was half empty, she had counted eight walk-in customers since she arrived.

"I opened up two years ago, and it was difficult to keep the business afloat at first, especially because I started off with a loan to cover the furnishing and reno-vations. The former owners of the shop did very poor maintenance, and I had to change a lot to make it presentable."

"Did you get the cafeteria on lease?" she asked, genuinely interested in talking about his business progress. It helped get her mind off waiting for Becky's arrival.

"No, it belonged to my grandmother. She rented it out when she closed down her diner, and I made use of it when I moved back to town. I got a loan and started the business, oblivious to how difficult it would get at some point.

"Was it a cooperate loan?"

Richard shook his head. "I got it from a relative."

"Oh…"

He looked at her half-empty mug, and he smiled. "I guess you enjoyed the tea."

"I did." A smile crossed her face. "Thanks."

"You're welcome," he replied, and rose to his feet.

The door opened, and Becky made her way into the cafeteria. She beamed and waved at Lucy, then cat-walked towards her.

"My friend is here," Lucy said as Richard gathered the mug and saucer.

"I'll see you around, Lucy."

He left as Becky arrived and took over his seat. "I see you've met Richard Lester... he's one of Ivy Creek's eligible bachelors," she said and eyed Richard at the counter. "If I was single, I might have snatched him up for myself."

Lucy eyed her, and Becky broke into a short laugh. "That was a joke, relax. Why did you want to meet?"

Lucy raked her fingers through her hair. "I need a list of the guests at the charity event you hosted last time. Every person in attendance that night, and also the team of ushers you hired for the job."

Becky's brows furrowed, and she lowered her purse to the table. "Why? Did something happen?"

"No, no," Lucy replied with a dismissive wave of her hand. "I would like to network with other businesses, and I know you have a lot of connections with the wealthy people of Ivy Creek," she stammered. "I just need a new client list."

"I can help with that," Becky replied in an enthusiastic tone. "Connecting people is what I do." Her eyes lit up, and she took out a notepad from her purse. She handed it over to Lucy with a pen. "Write down your email address, and I will send it to you once I get to my laptop tonight."

"Thanks, Becky."

Lucy scribbled down her email address and slid the note back to Becky. Once she got the list, she would go through it, and try to find out each guest's relationship with the Wilsons. Becky snatched her purse from the table and glanced at the golden wristwatch on her left wrist.

"I have to go now," she said, and gave Lucy a sly smile. "You should give the young man your number. Seems like he can't take his eyes off you."

Lucy stole a glance in Richard's direction and their eyes met briefly. He smiled at her, winked, and then focused on the customer by the counter. She gathered her things and exited the cafeteria with Becky.

Lucy flagged down a cab after Becky drove away and rode back home thinking about her brief encounter with Richard Lester. She wondered if he was truly interested in her, as Becky speculated, or if he was simply a playboy.

*T*ricia's car was missing from the corner of the building when Lucy arrived at the bakery.

Inside the kitchen, Hannah hummed to the music playing through her AirPods as Lucy entered the bakery and took off her coat. She unwrapped her shawl next and rolled the sleeves of her sweater up before walking over to the counter.

Hannah flashed a grin. "We had two customers today," she announced in a cheery tone. "I feel relaxed now."

Lucy saw the corners of Hannah's eyes lift as she smiled, and she shrugged off the heaviness weighing down on her and reached for a napkin.

"It's a good thing," Lucy replied as she folded the napkin. "Everything will get better," she added. "Where is Aunt Tricia?"

"She went off to get some items from the grocery store."

Lucy checked the display glass and counted the pastries they had left. They would make a new batch of bread tomorrow, and hopefully, more customers would come by. Lucy hoped she could put the entire ordeal of the Wilsons' death behind her and move forward.

A lady walked into the bakery holding her daughter as Lucy finished counting the remaining cupcakes and Hannah greeted her.

"Welcome to Sweet Delights. What would you like?"

"Do you have an apple pie?" the lady asked and turned to her daughter.

The little girl stared at the cupcakes on display and Lucy saw her eyes widen.

"What would you like, sweetie?" her mother asked, running a hand over the girl's blonde pigtail braids.

"Uhhhm…" she licked her lips and lifted her saucer round eyes to Lucy's. Her cheek colored, and she glanced at the display glass again. "I want… I don't know what I want," she exclaimed in a tiny, unsure voice.

"You should try our cupcakes," Lucy chirped in, and signaled to Hannah to get the lady's pie packed while she helped the little girl make a choice. "The sprinkles are amazing, and we have different flavors and blends too."

The girl jumped and tugged at her mother's hand. "I want the cupcakes then," she sang out, giggling. "Mom, I'll have two cupcakes please, the ones with the sprinkles."

"Alright, Zoey." The lady giggled, and Lucy shot her an amused look. "She learned how to pedal her bike on her own today, so she's really excited."

"That's amazing, Zoey. Learning to pedal on your own is an achievement."

Zoey flashed Lucy a wide smile, showcasing her set of white teeth. "I know," she replied, swinging her arms. "My dad taught me, and he promised to let me ride at the park once winter is over. It will be so much fun."

"I'm sure it will be," Lucy replied, and Hannah returned with a package. Lucy wrapped Zoey's cupcakes and added an extra piece. "I've added an extra for you to try out with your dad," she said and handed over the pack to Zoey's mother.

"Thanks," Zoey said, and spun around. She jogged towards the door singing a popular children's rhyme, *Twinkle, Twinkle, Little Star*. Her mother chuckled, and paid for the items in cash, waving at Hannah and Lucy before walking out of the store.

Zoey reminded Lucy of when she learned to ride her bicycle and she shook her head, smiling to herself as a memory of her riding in the park with her father flashed through her mind. "She's cute," she whispered, and turned to Hannah.

Hannah dusted her hands together. "We've run out of cupcakes and chips."

Lucy walked around the counter and took a seat. She spread her legs out in front of her and sat upright when Richard Lester crossed her mind. She hadn't seen him around town before, and when Becky had mentioned *Lou's Café*, a mental image of some old barista crossed her mind.

"I dropped by *Lou's Café* today. It's a lovely place with beautiful scenery, and I met Richard Lester for the first time. He's a charming young man."

"Richard Lester?" Hannah rasped. She scoffed and shook her head. "He's charming sure, and he's got honeyed words."

Lucy caught the cynicism in Hannah's venom laced words.

"You know him well?"

"He used to date my sister," she replied. Lucy's ears perked up as she listened to Hannah.

"They got along as friends at first when he moved into town two years ago. We all thought he was perfect for her, but he strung her along and then acted like she didn't exist when he moved on to his next girl. He never commits to anything long term, that I can assure you."

Richard's genuine smile as he offered her a cup of tea flashed in her mind and also when he winked at her as she left his shop. She shook it away, amazed at the interesting twist of Hannah knowing him so well.

"How did you two meet, by the way?" Hannah asked, pulling Lucy out of her thoughts.

"I met with Becky at his café earlier today to get the list of guests at her party the night the Wilsons died."

"You suspect one of the guests might have had something to do with their poisoning?"

"Yes. Whoever poisoned them had to have access to the treats beforehand. Once Becky sends over the list, I will go through it and try to see how many of the guests have a personal relationship with them."

"That's a brilliant plan."

Hannah and Lucy continued their conversation, shifting from talking about Becky's guest list to updates on the concession she had set up close to the park four months ago. After her hired assistant, Diane, who ran the store, tendered her resignation last month, she had closed down the store.

Lucy hoped to reopen it once the Wilsons investigation was complete. Having a few customers at the bakery had renewed her passion for her business and ignited some hope that there was some light at the end of a very dark tunnel.

*I hope I keep getting customers like Zoey and her mother, who happen to care little for town gossip.*

She made plans with Hannah to reduce their daily stock, but include newer recipes, and as they mulled over new ideas, the door burst open. Her head whipped up and she spotted Bruce Wilson.

Lucy braced herself immediately as he marched towards her menacingly.

*B*ruce reached where Lucy stood, and color drained from her face as he stared at her.

*What do I do?*

Hannah scurried into the kitchen, leaving Lucy to face Bruce on her own, and Lucy's mind reeled with different thoughts. *Why was Bruce Wilson here? Did he hear the rumors? Or about the cops' investigation of her treats? And why had Hannah left her to confront him all by herself?*

"Bruce…" she began.

"I heard about what you did," he interrupted before she could finish her sentence. "It's commendable, and it's why I'm here."

*He wasn't here to fight her?* Lucy bit her lower lip and closed her eyes for a second, slowly exhaling to ease the pressure building in her chest. So he wasn't here because of his parents' murder? She blinked, and a shaky laugh escaped her lips. Her racing pulse slowed, and she clapped her hands. "Thank you, Bruce," she replied, and offered him a seat, even though she wasn't sure what he was talking about.

"I met with a close friend who works on the local business committee, and he recommended your treats for my expansion plans. He says you supplied the treats at the Andersons' charity event weeks ago."

"I did."

A satisfied smile crossed Bruce's lips, and he looked around the bakery. "You have a nice setup here, but I'm certain walk-in customers aren't enough to generate huge profits," he paused, and took out an envelope from the breast pocket of his blue shirt. "How about we work together?"

She took the envelope and ripped it open, reading through the brief words. "That's a grant I just got from the local bank, and it will cover all my expansion expenses. Working with me means you will have a sublet in my grocery stores where we can put your pastries on display for sale. Of course I'll be offering upfront payment for whatever supplies you bring, and I would need a lot to cover all my stores."

Her lips curved into a wide smile until the sides of her mouth hurt, then she muffled a squeal of excitement. "I... I would love to work with you, Bruce."

"Great! My assistant will contact you by next week to draw up a plan and please add whatever new ideas you have to the list."

"I sure will."

Bruce got up, gave her one last smile before walking out, and Lucy released a pent-up breath. He had seemed upset when he walked into the bakery, and for a minute, she feared he would accuse her of his parents' murder.

Hannah returned to the dining area and sat with Lucy. "What was that about?"

"Bruce offered a business deal," Lucy replied, still giddy with excitement at Bruce's news. "He wants me to supply his chain of grocery stores with pastries... we would have a sublet for our goods."

Hannah breathed out an easy laugh, and her eyes danced. "That's amazing!"

"I know, right," Lucy tittered, unable to control her joy. Ideas already bounced inside her head like tiny rubber balls, and she couldn't wait to get started on the new project.

"We should try perfecting the recipes for at least three new pastries to add to our current menu."

"First off, we should celebrate," Lucy replied. She went into the kitchen and returned seconds later with a bottle of sparkling grape wine and two glasses.

"To more good news," Hannah toasted as their glasses clinked. They drank and continued discussing the recipes when Tricia returned. She drifted through the doors and joined them, slipping into the conversation easily about Bruce.

Bruce's determination to expand the store regardless of the murder investigation of his parents was a powerful move, and she couldn't settle the tiny sprout of envy in her heart. *I wish I could focus more, and not allow any circumstance to derail me.*

"Bruce Wilson wants to work with us on his expansion," Hannah said.

"It's true," Lucy said when her aunt turned to her. "We would supply his grocery stores pastries."

Tricia sipped her wine and cocked her head to one side. She grinned and reached for the bottle again. "This definitely calls for a celebration."

They toasted again, and minutes later, Hannah said her goodbyes as her shift had ended. Lucy and Tricia stayed in the bakery longer before retiring to the apartment upstairs. As Lucy prepared for bed, she thought about Bruce's proposal again.

Gigi strolled over to where she sat and she picked her up. "We are doing better, Gigi," she whispered, and Gigi purred.

"We got a new business deal, and things are looking good." She stroked Gigi's fur repeatedly, enjoying the fluffiness.

Gigi was fast asleep in a minute, and Lucy gently placed her in the snug bed by the corner of the room and switched off the light. She dropped on her bed and pulled the sheets over her body and snuggled into her pillows.

She couldn't wait to start on Bruce Wilson's order, and she hoped the outcome of this job would differ from the disappointment of the lost orders in the past few weeks. *This is all I've got now.* Lucy planned to impress Bruce Wilson with her skills.

Her phone pinged on the dresser, and she reached for it. Becky's email flashed on the screen, and she sprang up. She positioned a pillow to support her back as she sat.

She hoped the email would lead her to something useful as she clicked it open and read the brief note attached to it.

*This is a list of the guests and the business or companies they run. I hope you find it useful... xoxo Becky.*

The first name on the list was Richard Lester.

$\mathcal{T}$he next morning, Lucy did not hear her phone's alarm buzzing. She snored lightly, dragging the sheets over her face to shield her eyes from the rays of dawn entering her room.

She finally stirred awake when something warm lapped at her feet, and she opened her eyes to see Gigi purring and licking her feet. Lucy groaned and sat up, ruffling her hair with both hands. She pushed stray strands away from her face and focused on Gigi.

"I need more sleep," she complained and searched the bed for her phone. It was past 7 a.m. She had overslept, missing the time for her early morning run. Lucy slipped out of the bed and stretched her arms out.

She spent half the night reading Becky's email, and interesting facts had popped up. The Wilsons not only owned two grocery stores in town, they also had buildings out on sublets, and one of them was 6 Dune Street. That was the exact location of Lou's Café where she met Becky.

Lucy couldn't remember seeing Richard at Becky's party

that night, but he had gotten an invitation, so why didn't he attend? Besides, Richard told her the building had belonged to his grandmother. *Was that a lie? What else did he lie about?*

Lucy began dressing up after a hot shower. She stepped into her navy-blue pants and slipped into a floral-patterned cream-colored shirt. She planned to drop by Becky's office that morning, and confirm for herself all she could about Richard Lester.

When she reached the kitchen, Aunt Tricia sat with a mug of hot cocoa, and she waved a newspaper in Lucy's direction. "Come join me, dear. Are you heading out?"

"Yes," Lucy replied, and sat down. "Can I borrow your car?" She picked a pancake from the plate on the table, and after taking a bite, she added. "I want to meet with Becky."

"Did something happen?"

Lucy shook her head. "I just need to confirm a few things with her," she replied.

"Sure, you can drive my car. The key is upstairs."

Lucy finished her pancake, helped herself to a cup of hot cocoa before stepping out of the bakery. She drove to Becky's office address and walked into the building, stopping by the reception to ask for directions.

"Walk down that corridor, and stop by the fourth door," the short, plump woman at the front desk pointed at Becky's office down the hall.

"Thanks," Lucy breathed, then followed the directions.

She knocked before twisting the knob. Lucy entered the office, and Mr. Anderson's smile greeted her.

"Lucy," he said, and stood up from his chair. "What a surprise visit."

She crossed over to the table and accepted his extended hand, smiling as she eased into the chair he offered. "I came in to check on Becky," she replied, and looked around the office.

The office had seamless windows and a breath-taking view of the lawn outside. A dark walnut colored bookcase lined the right-side wall, and on the left was an exquisite black rug that matched the two-seater couch in the corner.

"Unfortunately, Becky had to leave town this morning for a business meeting, but she should be back in a few hours," Roland replied. "Did you need something? I'll be glad to assist if I can."

Lucy contemplated asking him about Richard Lester. He represented most of the town's rich members, so he could provide answers to some of her questions. Roland raised a brow when she didn't reply immediately, and she flashed him a smile.

"Actually, you can be of help. I was contemplating working with some other businesses in town, and I would like your input on some of them. I have interest in Lou's Café, and I want to know if he owns the café or…"

"Richard Lester owns the café," Roland replied before she finished. "However, he doesn't run it on his own, the Wilsons do."

"I don't understand."

"Richard is a nephew of Mr. Wilson, and he took a loan years back to start up the business. Rumors say he didn't pay back in time, and that led them to have some issues, but I represented Mr. Wilson, and I know for a fact that he cared little about a few thousand dollars his nephew borrowed to run a cafeteria."

*So, Richard didn't lie about owning the building.*

"Was he at the party that night? I don't remember seeing him."

Roland nodded his reply and picked a wrapped candy from the tray on the table. Lucy watched him pop it into his mouth and chew.

Lucy studied him, and she noticed how he toyed with a

fancy colored candy he picked from the side of the table, and a grin broke out on his face, but his lower lip quivered as he looked at his hands.

"I have a sweet tooth," he explained. "Becky always complains about it, but it doesn't stop my cravings. I will definitely be popping into Sweet Delights one of these days."

"I appreciate that," Lucy replied. "It's nice to have someone compliment my work considering people fear my cupcakes had something to do with the Wilsons' death."

Roland's brows creased, and he wrinkled his nose in a worried expression. "That must be so difficult," he sympathized. "I believe you're innocent, and anyone with an ounce of sense would think so too."

"Thank you, Roland. It means a lot that you think so."

He nodded his agreement. "Keep working hard, and Sweet Delights could grow to be the premier bakery in the state of Colorado."

Lucy hoped that would happen one day, too. She thanked Roland for his time and left the building. She sped down the road, taking the first right turn that would lead to a connecting road taking her to the highway.

She slowed when her phone beeped, and she accepted the call from her smart watch.

"Hey, Lucy, where are you?" Hannah's tense voice floated through the speaker, and Lucy stopped when she spotted the red traffic light.

"I had something to take care of, but I'm driving to the bakery right now. Is there a problem? Do you need something?"

"Mr. Wilson's here," Hannah replied. Her voice trembled as she added. "Please get back fast."

The call ended, and Lucy felt an ominous feeling wash over her. *Why was Bruce Wilson at her bakery again? What did he want this time?*

She pressed down the accelerator and zoomed onto the highway, heading to the bakery. *What if Bruce found out about the presumptions surrounding my treats and he is there to cancel our contract? What do I do next?*

## 13

*L*ucy was surprised at what greeted her when she walked into the bakery. It wasn't a snarling, angry man who wanted to rip apart the contract they had agreed to. It was a more tentative man who was pacing the dining area. And it wasn't Bruce Wilson. It was his brother, Wayne. She took off her coat, handed it over to Hannah, and walked over to him. *Thank God, it isn't Bruce;* she thought.

"Mr. Wilson," she called. He turned around to face her. His sharp, irritated gaze swept up her face, and Lucy held her breath in anticipation. "Did you need something?"

Wayne brushed back his hair and straightened his spine. "Lucy," he replied, eyeing her. "I got news about my parents' investigation from the detectives. They died from poisoning…" he paused and glared at her. "Food poisoning."

Lucy remained quiet, counting the seconds until the accusation came. "I saw them eat your cupcakes at the Andersons' charity party the night they were hospitalized."

His words crashed on her, and Lucy sucked in a deep breath, trying to stop her panic. "Wayne…" she whispered, but he raised a hand, silencing her.

"You killed them? You poisoned those cupcakes... and I will make sure you pay for that," he yelled. "I will make sure you pay," he repeated.

"Wayne, please listen to me," Lucy tried again. Her temples pulsed, and out of the corner of her eye, she saw a woman and her daughter leave their seats. "I had nothing to do with it... The cops are..."

"Liar," he accused again. "I can't believe a word you say," he added in a quivering voice. Lucy saw tears pool in his eyes before he looked away from her, and she swallowed against the tightness in her throat.

*Did Wayne really believe she poisoned his parents? Why would he think she did? Did everyone in town also doubt her innocence?*

A woman walked into the bakery and rushed to Wayne's side. "Come on, honey," she said.

Lucy pressed her lips together, and the woman shot her an apologetic stare.

"Please, Wayne, let's go outside," she cooed.

Wayne hesitated at first, before walking out of the bakery with the woman. Lucy staggered backwards, unable to hold her weight with her wobbly feet.

Hannah rushed to steady her, and Lucy leaned against her. She couldn't take any more of these accusations and attacks on her business. The detectives still had no news, and she remained patient because she trusted they could get to the real culprit.

"What do I do?" she asked Hannah as they walked over to a chair. Lucy slouched into it and buried her head in her palms. "I need to do something. Today it's just Wayne Wilson. It might be someone else accusing me of murder tomorrow."

"You should reach out to Taylor," Hannah replied, and patted her shoulder. "He should have news about the sample testing by now. It's taken long enough."

The lady who led Wayne out walked back into the bakery. Hannah and Lucy turned to her, and she offered an apologetic smile.

"I'm so sorry," she muttered, crossing her fingers in front of her. "I'm Jane Wilson, and my husband was so out of line earlier."

"It's okay," Lucy replied. "I understand how he feels... it's a lot to lose both parents out of the blue."

"It's been so hard on him since they died, and he's..." she croaked, sniffed, and raised a finger to rub the corner of her eyes. "He's developed an anxiety issue... lots of anger outbursts like what happened earlier. I'm sorry for any inconvenience," she added, gave Lucy one last smile before walking away.

The bakery had emptied during the scene with Wayne, and Hannah walked around to gather the dishes on the tables. Lucy's chest was tight enough to explode, and she knew the one way she could get relief was to get answers.

"I have to see Taylor," she whispered, adjusted her purse on her shoulder, and hurried out of the bakery.

———

TAYLOR STOOD outside the station with another cop when Lucy arrived. She got out of her car and crossed over to him with determined steps. "Taylor," she called, and he turned to her. "We need to talk."

He whispered something to the cop, then walked over to her, slipping his hands into the pocket of his pants. "Lucy... Do you need something?" he asked in a cool tone.

Lucy swallowed and extended her clenched fists. "If you think I'm responsible for the Wilsons' death, then arrest me," she replied.

She saw him look at her outstretched fists, and Lucy

raised her chin, determined not to back down. He could either give her answers that would clear her name or arrest her as a suspect. Whichever way, she was not leaving without answers.

"I have no reason to arrest you," he said. "Investigations are still ongoing and more evidence came to light recently."

"More evidence?" she asked, her heart hammering in her chest. "What... What evidence?"

*Please let this be something positive.*

"Your treats did not contain any poisonous substance, so you didn't do it," he said, and Lucy exhaled. Her lower lip quivered, and she wiped her sweaty forehead with her forearm.

"We are still testing other samples of what the Wilsons had that night, their drink, and food samples we collected from their house. The forensic team will determine which of those items contained the poison."

Lucy placed a hand over her chest. "So this means I'm free?" she asked, her tone light. Taylor shook his head, and she frowned. "What else?"

"You should be careful henceforth," he replied. "The killer is still out there, and whoever it is, they are trying to pin it on you."

Lucy's blood chilled, and she blinked. *Why would anyone want to frame me? I have no connections to the Wilsons or any rich resident of Ivy Creek.*

"Why would anyone do that?" she breathed out.

Taylor shrugged. "Beats me... just make sure you are careful," he added.

## 14

"*L*et's get some gas," Tricia said, and swerved her car into the gas station by the highway. Lucy got out of the passenger's seat and walked over to the stand while Tricia wandered into the fuel station's store.

Lucy filled the tank and sat in the driver's seat to wait for Tricia. It was the first Sunday in the month, and Tricia's house renovation was complete. They drove downtown to inspect the work done, and the changes satisfied Tricia.

Lucy especially liked the landscape of the front lawn. The daisies gave the air a sweet scent, and Lucy already imagined having Thanksgiving dinner at her house. They could host a small get-together in the front yard just like her parents did and invite friends over.

A white truck pulled into the station and parked by the empty pump. Lucy saw Bruce Wilson get out from the driver's seat, and he waved when he spotted her.

"Hey," he said when he got to where she sat. "It's good I found you here. I planned to visit your bakery this evening to apologize about my brother's behavior the last time… I heard about what happened."

Lucy groaned. She couldn't believe her brief altercation with Wayne had gotten on to the Ivy Creek rumor mill.

"No apologies necessary," she replied. "I understand what your family is going through, and I hope the cops get to the truth soon."

"Yeah, me too."

"How are you coping with your grief?" she asked. Bruce quirked a brow up, and she quickly added. "I mean... you seem alright, and more business focused than your brother. I just thought that it should be hard on you too."

"It is," he replied, and his countenance changed. "I've known my parents all my life and being without them is difficult. I distract myself with work. It's why it might come off like I'm not grieving. I know it gets easier with time, but I still dread going back home to an empty house, and knowing they aren't coming back. I wonder what it will be like this Christmas without them," he added ruefully.

"You will get through it," she said, hoping her words offered a bit of comfort. "When my parents passed, everything reminded me of them, and it hurt, but it got easier."

Bruce blinked his puffy eyes and looked around, then back at her. "Did you get a call from my assistant?" he asked, changing the subject.

"No, not yet."

"I will make sure she gets back to you this week. I've made a list of the pastries I would like to have. You can list a few and run it by me before you begin production."

"That's perfect... looking forward to it," Lucy replied. He waved at her, then retreated to fill up his tank. Lucy watched him drive away when he finished, and she sighed.

*What's keeping you, Aunt Tricia,* she wondered.

Another car drove in, and Lucy admired the neat jet-black sedan. The door opened, and Richard Lester stepped down. He spotted her immediately, and the corner of his lips moved.

"I haven't seen you around," Richard said when he strolled over to her. "I hoped you would drop by because you could not stay away from my chamomile tea," he teased, and Lucy laughed.

His light laugh came easily, and Lucy noticed the dimple on his left cheek.

"How have you been?" he asked.

"I've been good, just getting around my usual activities. How are you holding up since your uncle, Mr. Wilson, just passed?"

His eyebrows flew towards his hairline and he raised a hand to stroke his clean-shaven chin. "How did you know he was my uncle?"

Lucy lifted a shoulder. "It's a small town, people talk. Besides, there's a striking resemblance between both of you."

Richard chortled. "I get that a lot," he replied and dropped his hand. "When my father died many years ago, my uncle took me in and treated me like a son. I loved being around him and my aunt so much, and he planned to let me run one of his grocery stores in town."

Lucy's ears perked up. She tapped her fingers on the steering wheel and asked. "So why didn't you?"

"Well, it seemed like there were some issues between his sons. They believed my uncle was being partial, and I didn't want to create any issues in the family, so I opted to start my own business. He gave me a loan, and I put the plans for Lou's Café in motion. But things didn't turn out well. He kept changing the terms of the loan to suit him, and I got fed up."

"What do you mean terms of the loan?"

"He increased the interest on the loan and made changes to the partnership contract I signed without notifying me. I wanted it to be over, so I promised to pay him back all I owed, and close the café, but unfortunately, he passed away before I could.

His face sagged, and his voice turned hoarse as he continued. "It's been a mess since he died, I must confess. I'm getting pulled in every corner by extended family members, and the cops trying to investigate. I had to close my shop on Friday because the sheriff summoned me to the station for interrogation."

Lucy held back the urge to batter him with more questions. She pressed her lips together, and Richard gulped in air, releasing it intermittently before looking at her again. "I think maybe it's time to close up and move on to something else," he whispered.

"You shouldn't give up," she replied, and reached out to touch his arm. Lucy spotted her aunt walking over to them, and she withdrew.

"I'll see you around, Lucy," Richard said, and walked away.

Tricia reached for Lucy and handed over the shopping bags she held.

"Why did you take so long?" Lucy asked as she entered her side of the car.

Tricia grinned while Lucy started the engine. "The salesman was fun to chat with," she replied, and turned to Lucy. "Who was the young man I saw you flirting with?" she asked in an amused tone.

"I wasn't flirting," Lucy said. Her cheeks gained color as Tricia chuckled and teased her with her look. "He's Richard Lester, Mr. Wilson's nephew, and I was trying to get any information I could about his relationship with the Wilsons."

"Did you find anything?" Tricia asked and took the turn leading to the bakery. "He is a fine young man. What reason would he have to kill his uncle?"

She replayed her conversation with Richard in her head, and Taylor's warning flashed through her mind. *I think someone is trying to pin this murder on you.*

"I don't know," she replied, and stared outside the window. Richard had seemed distraught as he talked about his uncle's death, and she didn't know if she could trust his reaction.

*Is he the broken man she talked to? Or is he just desperate enough to do something extreme to get his way?*

She didn't know what to believe about either Richard or Bruce or Wayne.

"He has a reason to want his uncle dead," Lucy whispered, and Tricia looked in her direction. "He took a loan, and he told me Mr. Wilson kept changing the terms without his consent.

"There was tension between them before he died, and on the night of the party Richard Lester was there," she continued. "I don't remember seeing him but Mr. Anderson confirmed his presence that night. Bruce is overly ambitious, that's probable cause. Wayne feels over-looked, and Richard thinks they extorted him. It could be any of them."

Tricia said nothing, and the unanswered question of the killer's identity hung in the air.

She spent the rest of the night replaying her conversations with Bruce, Wayne, and Richard.

There was no evidence to back her suspicions about any of the men. She thought for a moment and took her phone to go through the list Becky sent her again.

Halfway through it, a thought occurred to Lucy for the first time. *What if it was some other business partner?*

---

## 15

*T*he next morning, Lucy's phone beeped twice on the table in her bakery. She snatched it, took the call and lifted it to her ear, hoping to hear good news.

She and Hannah had emailed most of the business owners on Becky's list the previous day and anyone interested could reach her through her contact address, but so far, they had gotten no response yet.

"Hello," Lucy spoke into the receiver, and held her breath, waiting for the person on the other end to speak up.

The voice on the other end mumbled something in Spanish, and Lucy frowned. "Hello?"

She sighed and dropped the call when the caller continued to speak Spanish. "Probably a wrong number," she whispered when she met Hannah's expectant gaze.

"Try calling Becky," Hannah suggested. "She could speak to the business owners directly, and I think they will respond better to her."

"That's a brilliant idea."

Lucy dialed Becky's number, toying with the hem of her blouse as she waited for the call to connect. It rang through to voicemail thrice, and she dropped the phone. "It keeps ringing to voicemail," she said.

"Maybe drop by her office? She might be too busy to take your calls."

Lucy picked up her notepad and stared at the list of contacts she had scribbled down. Becky could help her connect to these people effortlessly. "I will drop by her office."

Minutes later, she was driving past Lou's Café and heading towards Becky Anderson's office downtown. Three cops stood outside the building, and Lucy wondered what they talked about as she walked in.

Becky welcomed Lucy with a huge grin when she walked into the office. "How are you doing?"

"I'm great," Lucy replied, and took a seat. "I called earlier, but it rang straight to voice mail, so I dropped by."

Becky glanced at her phone on the table. She picked it up and flashed her an apologetic smile. "I'm so sorry. I'm swamped with organizing deals and I didn't hear it ring."

"It's fine," Lucy said with a smile. "I sent out business proposals to the people on the list you gave me, and I was hoping you could introduce me to them in person or put in a good word, so they read my proposal."

She opened her purse and handed over the list she had emailed. "Here is a list of those I contacted."

"Alright," Becky replied, accepting the notepad. She glanced at it and dropped it on the table. "I will place a call to each of them during the weekend when I have some time, and I will make sure they consider your proposal.

"Thanks Becky, I really appreciate this." Lucy looked around the office, and noticed the pile of books on the couch by the corner. A black suit jacket draped over the couch, and a pair of black shoes lay neatly by the corner of the rug.

"You had a guest?" Lucy asked, pointing at the couch.

"They're Roland's," she replied. "He works here often and sometimes receives guests."

"Oh..." Lucy rose to her feet.

"Let's meet on Monday so I can update you on my progress," Becky suggested and picked up her glasses from the table.

———

LUCY ARRIVED at Sweet Delights before she realized she left her notepad in Becky's office.

She had some recipes she was perfecting written in the notebook, and she needed it for the weekend.

Lucy flagged down a cab and instructed the driver to take her back to Becky's office. When the cab arrived, she jumped out and darted towards the building.

She was almost out of breath as she rushed in through the door. "I left my notepad."

"Right." Becky gathered her items from the table as she spoke. "I got a call from one of the business owners on your list minutes after you left, and he's agreed to meet and hear me out. I need to meet with him right now. Your notepad is somewhere on my table... I'll be back in a few minutes."

"Oh, that's fine. I'll wait," Lucy replied as Becky slipped into her green stilettos and patted her cheeks.

"How do I look?"

Lucy raised her right thumb. "Perfect."

Becky sashayed out of the office with a smile, shutting the door with a loud thud, and Lucy sighed. She looked around the place, and the huge mahogany bookshelf on the left wall caught her attention.

The bookshelf had three sections. They displayed awards in the lowest section, and the other two contained books.

She picked up an award for a promising firm in the state, admired it before replacing it gently on the shelf.

She looked in the books section and landed on a misaligned book jutting out. She reached for it, opened the first page, and read the notes.

*Lou's Café figures.*

Lucy scanned the pages of the book, her fingers tracing out the debit and credit balance on each page. Richard mentioned the skyrocketing interest on the loan he took from Mr. Wilson, and she wondered if Roland kept records of everything concerning the businesses he handled like this.

She noticed every month had the same closing balance, and that didn't seem right. The same closing balance could only mean there was no profit at the end of the month. If Lou's Café didn't make any profits, then how did Richard survive after paying off his loan?

Lucy froze, and she nearly screamed out in shock when the door burst open and a voice boomed.

"What do you think you're doing?"

## 16

*L*ucy's hands turned cold and clammy. As Roland stepped forward, Lucy saw something flash in his icy blue eyes.

*Was it anger? Or fear?* She couldn't tell the difference because he masked it with a grin that resembled a sneer.

"You shouldn't go through people's stuff. What do you have behind you?" he asked.

Lucy shifted until she collided with the shelf. Pain radiated through her back at the point of contact, and she bit her lower lip to keep from yelping. There was something different about the way Roland looked at her. The grin on his face disappeared and was replaced with a thick glare that made her shiver.

"I was reading a book," she replied in a tiny voice, her heartbeat racing. Lucy swallowed. "I wasn't snooping around. Becky asked me to wait, and I didn't know you were here. I should leave," she added hurriedly. Roland took three long strides and grabbed the hand at her back.

"You're a terrible liar," he snarled and snatched the book

from her. "I could see this book behind you the entire time," he added, his grip still tight on her arm.

"You're hurting me," Lucy whimpered. She rubbed her arm when he released her and glared at him. "Fine, you caught me... I found the book on the shelf, and I was going through the numbers. Turns out they don't add up... the interest Richard pays don't reflect in the books," she accused. "What did you do?"

Roland burst into a cackle. He flung his head back as his laugh rocked his entire body. "You still don't get it, do you?" he asked when he stopped.

"You drove a wedge between Mr. Wilson and his nephew," she repeated, wondering what else he did.

Roland sneered. "Oh, come on Lucy... I didn't do anything that hasn't been done before. We live in a world where the rich get richer, and the poor get poorer. It's a known principle, and as a businesswoman, you should know that."

She watched him, her insides recoiling in fear as he paced the room. He rolled up his sleeves, unknotted his tie, and turned back to her.

"A sales offer for Lou's Café came in a while back. The investors wanted to pay a huge sum to get the building, and still allow Mr. Wilson to have shares in whatever business they used the place for. It was good business, the best deal anyone could get, but he turned down the offer because his nephew had built a business there."

He paused and pointed a finger at her. "A business he couldn't keep afloat."

"You increased the rates of the interest and the terms of payment. How did you expect him to keep up?" Lucy asked. "He thought his uncle did that. He had a hard time because of it, and you think you did nothing wrong?"

Lucy saw him assess her. She shook her head. *How could*

*he lack such human decency? Lying to his client and falsifying ledgers was a crime.*

"I told Wilson about the deal long before Richard came to town, but he didn't listen. I gave him a lot of reasons to make that deal and he promised to think about it, but the minute his nephew came to town, he jumped at that offer. Don't you see what he did wrong?"

"No, I don't," Lucy replied defiantly.

His nostrils flared, and he scoffed. "You're just like them, aren't you? You think you're better than everyone else with your self-righteous attitude." Roland lunged for her, and she couldn't escape because he backed her into a corner.

He gripped her shoulders and shook her hard. "I worked hard for Wilson and when I needed him to do just one thing for me, he refused. All he had to do was take the offer, and they would compensate us handsomely, but he was stubborn."

"So, you killed him?" Lucy yelled.

Roland struck her cheek hard. It stung, and tears welled in her eyes as she staggered away from him. He followed quickly, yanking her by her hair when she tried to get away from him.

"You're right, I did," he growled. His large hands circled her neck, clamping down on her throat so she couldn't speak. Lucy whimpered. She struggled against him, her hands pinching his skin.

*I want to live;* she thought as she struggled to breathe. His crazed gaze remained steady on hers, his lips curved, exposing his teeth. *Please,* she tried to speak as she slowly slipped out of consciousness.

"I'm sorry, Lucy," she heard him say as she blacked out. "But some things have to stay as secrets."

## 17

*A* loud beep cut through her unconscious mind, jarring her out of the darkness, and Lucy opened her eyes wide.

She choked, her chest tightened as she struggled to breathe, and it was like Roland's hands were around her neck again. *Help me... someone please.*

Lucy tried to move her hands, but she couldn't. She floated in her surroundings, trying to find a balance amongst the beeps and noises in the background.

*What happened? How did I get here?*

Images of her struggle with Roland Anderson flashed in her mind, and her heart rate sped up. A nurse rushed into the room, and Lucy realized the continuous beeping monitor was connected to her arm.

The door opened again and Tricia and Hannah rushed in, each taking a side of the bed.

"Oh, God, Lucy. What happened?" Hannah said.

"Can you hear me? It's alright, you're in a hospital, and you'll be fine," Tricia cried, and Hannah latched on to her hand.

Lucy's chest tightened, her throat burned, and she tried to speak. Tears slid down her cheeks at the failed attempt, and Hannah reached out to wipe them.

"You'll be fine."

She nodded frantically and took in her surroundings. The nurse adjusted the IV fluids connected to her arm and walked out of the room. Lucy looked out of the window blinds and saw Becky.

Becky was sobbing with her face in her hands, her shoulders heaving up and down. She saw Becky briefly raised her head, mumble some words to the man by her side, and break down in tears again. Aunt Tricia reached for the blinds, pulling them closed.

Lucy's head suddenly spun as another wave of dizziness hit her. Her eyelids fluttered closed as the darkness called, and she slipped out again.

———

WHEN SHE OPENED HER EYES, Taylor was looking down at her.

"Hey," he whispered, and Lucy blinked.

"Hi," she croaked. She swallowed, hoping to ease some of the dryness in her throat, and she raised a hand to her neck.

"You sustained bruises and swollen airways. You speaking is a good sign."

She managed a faint laugh and dropped her hand to her side. "My aunt?" she asked when she noticed they were alone in the room. "Hannah?"

"They went to the station for questioning. You've been out for a day, and you're lucky to be alive."

"How did I get here? Who found me?" she asked in a wobbly voice.

"Becky returned to her office just in time," he replied.

"Roland Anderson had no way out of it because she called the cops immediately."

Lucy remembered seeing Becky crying outside, and her heart sank a little. She had admired Roland, and she knew Becky had loved him.

"We're still investigating, and we'll know the entire truth soon. You just need to hang in there and get better."

"I will," Lucy whispered with a smile. "Thank you, Taylor."

A moment of silence passed between them, and he returned the smile, the side of his mouth quirking up a little. "It's nothing... I was just doing my job."

Taylor got up and walked to the door. He glanced back and added. "You were brave, Lucy, and I never doubted your innocence."

Lucy chuckled when he left and sighed. The burden of the Wilsons' death no longer pressed on her conscience, and she was certain everything could only get better from here.

She fell asleep again after a nurse came in to check on her, and by evening she was feeling strong enough to sit up in her bed. Hannah dropped by with her aunt again, and they were laughing at a joke when Richard Lester walked into the room.

Tricia and Hannah excused themselves, grinning, and he took a seat by her bedside.

"I heard you almost died," he said. "You should be more careful, Lucy."

He reached over, patting her hand on the bed and Lucy's insides warmed.

"Are you alright?" she asked him, studying his face. He must have heard about Roland's deceit by now, she thought. *I wonder how he feels.*

Richard sucked in a deep breath. "I'm hanging in there," he replied. "I've been to the station twice today, and they told me everything. Roland added the numbers to the loan because he wanted to scare me off the property. It makes sense now... my uncle wouldn't have changed the terms without consulting me.

"When I confronted him, he denied it at first, but I didn't believe him. Turns out it was all part of Roland's manipulative scheme to run me out of town so he could sell off to some rich investor."

"I'm sorry you had to go through that," she whispered.

"Yeah... me too," he paused, and lifted a finger to touch her cheek. "I'm glad you didn't die, Lucy."

Lucy nodded.

He shifted in his chair. "I'll see you around."

"Yeah."

Her aunt returned to the room seconds after Richard left, and she had a teasing smile on. "He's into you, I can tell," she said.

Lucy shook her head. "He's not my type," she replied, laughing, and Tricia patted her shoulder playfully.

"Time will tell."

Lucy didn't agree with her aunt on that note. No matter how charming Richard Lester was, Hannah had told her of his past, and she was not looking to get hurt by any man. "I'll find the right man one day. Don't you worry," she replied and hugged her aunt.

For now, she was just relieved that the pandemonium of the last few weeks was over.

## 18

## TWO WEEKS LATER

"*C*heers," Lucy said and clicked her glass to Hannah's, then Tricia's. "To many more orders and paychecks." They laughed, and she sipped from her glass. "I'll bring the cake."

Lucy wandered into the kitchen and returned with the cream frosted cake. She cut into it, and served everyone a piece, then settled on her seat to eat her slice.

"We got three new orders from the proposal emails you sent out, and Bruce called to commend our work. He says he'll need a new batch of orders by next week," Lucy said.

Lucy was glad things were returning to normal. It had been discovered that Roland had poisoned the drinks of the Wilsons on the night of the charity gala. He knew they both loved sweet things and whoever served nibbles on the day would be a key suspect. He had slipped some poison pills into drinks he had offered them. His intention was to kill Mr. Wilson but since he wasn't sure if he would take the poisoned glass, he had spiked both drinks. Taylor had assured her that there was enough evidence to get him sent to jail for a very long time.

"I'm happy," Hannah beamed. "I knew business would bloom again, and now you can reopen the concession," she suggested.

"I will interview new candidates for the position," Lucy replied.

Halfway into their celebration, Becky walked into the bakery.

"Excuse me," Lucy said to Hannah and Tricia.

She led Becky out to the patio and sat with her. It snowed heavily earlier in the day and melting snow covered her front lawn. She noticed that the car Becky had driven to the bakery was an unfamiliar one.

"Lucy..." Becky said as her voice trailed off, and she reached into her purse for a handkerchief. She wiped her nose and shut her eyes for a second. "I came here to apologize for everything," she added in a croaky voice. "I planned to visit earlier, but I couldn't find the right time... the investigation is over, and I couldn't put it off much longer."

"I'm alright, Becky," Lucy replied, hating to see Becky so distraught. When they first met, she thought Becky was a snob, but now, she was more empathetic. "You shouldn't apologize."

Tears filled Becky's eyes, and she shuddered. Lucy reached for her hand on the table and squeezed it.

"It's water under the bridge," she added.

"I can't believe Roland did such a thing," she said, dabbing at her eyes. "We've been in debt for a while because of his gambling habit, and he told me he had it under control. He told me he had settled everything, and I shouldn't worry, and I didn't.... I should have known he was up to something," she continued.

"You didn't know, Becky. Don't beat yourself up... it was Roland's crime, not yours. He poisoned them... that's not on you."

"I'm lost and alone. I didn't know who I married. They are charging him with murder, and I might never see him again."

Lucy understood Becky's pain, and she wished she could help her. Becky always offered help when she needed it, and she wanted to do the same. She moved her chair closer to Becky's and wrapped her arms around her shoulders.

"You'll be fine, Becky. Trust me, you'll get through this."

Becky sobbed in her arms for a while. Minutes later, she pulled away and wiped her face. "I'm sorry," she apologized with a nervous laugh.

Lucy shook her head. "It's fine."

Becky rose to her feet and picked her bag from the table. "I should go."

"You could join us inside for a celebration," Lucy invited, hoping company would help lift her mood. "I want to help you feel better before you go, so please, come in," she offered.

She pleaded again when she noticed Becky's reluctance. "Please?"

"I don't want to intrude."

"You're not intruding," Lucy corrected and took her hand. "Come in and have a drink and some cake. I promise you'll feel better afterwards."

Becky entered the bakery with her. Hannah brought her a glass and a plate for the cake and she joined in the celebration.

As they talked and laughed, Lucy was glad she had made a new friend, despite all the pandemonium that had engulfed her world and taken her on a whirlwind ride of disappointment, rejection and redemption. Things were returning to normal and with the holiday season on the horizon, she was looking forward to the rest of the year. She had some great recipe ideas she couldn't wait to share with Ivy Creek.

## The End

# AFTERWORD

Thank you for reading Twinkle, Twinkle, Deadly Sprinkles. I really hope you enjoyed reading it as much as I had writing it!

If you have a minute, please consider leaving a review on Amazon or the retailer where you got it.

**Many thanks in advance for your support!**

# EAT ONCE, DIE TWICE

## CHAPTER 1 SNEAK PEEK

# ABOUT EAT ONCE, DIE TWICE

**Released**: November 2021
**Series**: Book 3 – Ivy Creek Cozy Mystery Series
**Standalone**: Yes
**Cliff-hanger**: No

**The third book in the Ivy Creek cozy mystery series.**

It seems Lucy has finally gotten the hang of running a bakery and serving the good citizens of Ivy Creek. She knows she has a lot to learn but she's up for the challenge. She just never bargained for competition from a new couple in town.

When one half of this dubious couple is found dead, Lucy is torn between minding her own business or helping the grieving person find justice for their loss.

Matters aren't helped when it appears all circumstantial and testimonial evidence points to this person as the killer.

But Lucy knows what it's like to be falsely accused in the court of public opinion.

Will she unearth the secrets that surround a building in town that seems linked to the murder?

Will she find out why the accused has so much to hide even though they've professed their innocence?

Will she help to find a killer that doesn't want to be found and restore normalcy to her life and small town?

Discover how Lucy helps to solve another intriguing murder in the latest book in this exciting series.

# CHAPTER 1 SNEAK PEEK

*L*ucy loved new things. And as she looked through her window at the golden, orange, green and brown leaves that were gently swaying on the tree outside, it was evident a new season had rolled by. This new season deserved a new look, and she was feeling brave to try something different. Staring at herself in the mirror, she wondered if she had made the right decision.

Her shoulder length brunette hair had grown a few inches over the past month, and she decided to keep the length as part of her current style.

She angled her head and got a clearer view of her face in the mirror. The platinum color suited her pale skin, but she wasn't sure it made her brown eyes pop.

"How do I look, Gigi?" she asked her Persian white cat.

Gigi purred and rubbed her fur on Lucy's feet. Lucy chuckled and ran her fingers through her hair.

"Is it too light?"

She sighed and turned away from the mirror, walking out of her room to the bakery downstairs, leaving Gigi behind.

Her employee, Hannah, sat in the kitchen alone, holding a

mug of hot chocolate in one hand, and a magazine in the other. She lifted her eyes from the magazine when Lucy entered the kitchen.

"Oh my God, Lucy, what did you do to your hair?" she asked with an amused laugh. "You weren't kidding when you mentioned changing your hair color. I didn't think you'd go through with it though."

Lucy shrugged. "I wanted a change. Experimenting with a new color seemed like a good idea," she replied and poured herself a glass of lemonade.

"Do I look good? Or is it too light? I applied the color and dozed off."

Hannah was a natural blonde, and another pair of eyes would confirm if she needed to find the nearest hair salon to undo her decision.

"It's lovely," Hannah replied, assessing her. "It really does suit you."

Lucy tucked strands of her hair behind her ear, and Hannah slid the magazine she held towards Lucy. "The annual Creek's Christmas fair," she said out loud. "Registration starts soon. This is a chance for Sweet Delights to share our pastries with a new clientele. There will be lots of foreign tourists at the fair," Hannah explained.

Lucy had never attended the Annual Christmas Fair because it was an event introduced after she moved out of town three years ago, but it was a brilliant idea. She imagined it would be an excellent opportunity for various businesses to display their products and make massive sales.

"We should try registering once it begins," Hannah said.

Lucy closed the magazine. "Yes, it's a good idea," she agreed. "We have lots of customers, and this fair will help raise more revenue to open one more sublet next year."

A banging noise from across the street caught Lucy's attention, and she walked over to the window to peek outside. The ongoing reconstruction had spanned a few weeks, and Lucy wondered what business would occupy the space once it was completed.

Hannah came over to where she stood. "It used to be a restaurant, but the owners sold out weeks before you moved back into town. I think a new designer boutique will take its place," she said.

Lucy noticed the brick walled patterns on the new walls and the humongous sized windows. She imagined that only a designer boutique would require such enormous windows.

The door swung open and Lucy walked over to the counter where a customer stood.

"Hi, welcome to Sweet Delights. What would you like?" she said.

The lady adjusted her tote bag on her shoulder. She scanned the counter for a second and finally made a choice. "I'll have the banana nut bread."

"That will be four dollars, and seventy-five scents, please."

She paid in cash, and as she walked out, two more customers walked in. Hannah attended to one, and Lucy took an order from the other person for six cupcakes. She added an extra to the order since the woman was a regular and wrapped them up in a fancy bag.

"Here you go," Lucy said. "Eighteen bucks for everything."

"Your items are always so pricey," the woman complained as she reached for her wallet. "I spend a lot on your cupcakes every week because my twins decide not to have anything else for brunch."

Lucy grinned. "Sweet Delights serves only the best because we know only the best come to Sweet Delights," she said as she winked at the lady. The lady chuckled and left the bakery with a smile on her face.

Lucy exhaled and cleaned some fingerprints off the counter.

"It's the first day of the week and we're out of banana bread and chocolate chip cookies," Hannah said. "We still have orders to fulfill by the end of the week, and we're almost out of flour."

Lucy hopped with excitement and counted the rest of the cupcakes in the display glass. This meant they had to produce more for the rest of the week. "We could make them tomorrow," she replied, after noting twenty cupcakes left.

She scratched her ears as loud scrapes and creaks echoed from the construction site across the road. Lucy stepped outside the bakery to get a better view of the work in progress.

She sat down on a chair, enjoying the cool afternoon breeze. It ruffled against her hair and she caught a whiff of her jasmine-scented shampoo.

A young boy stood by the corner of her mailbox dispensing fliers to anyone walking past. He stopped two women heading to her bakery and handed over fliers to them.

"Hey," Lucy called out in a loud voice to get the boy's attention.

His eyes popped wide as he spun around, and he fled down the street before she could say anything else. Her brows creased as she watched him disappear down an alley.

Lucy welcomed both women, who entered the bakery with warm smiles.

"Hi, Lucy," one of the ladies with a red beret greeted.

Lucy recognized her as a regular customer of Sweet Delights. She dropped by every afternoon and always ordered cheesecakes.

"Have you heard about the new bakery coming to town? Sounds exciting, doesn't it?"

"New bakery?" Lucy repeated.

"Right across the street from you. They're advertising all

around town," she replied, and pointed toward the construction site across the road.

Lucy's jaw dropped for a second as the ladies proceeded into the bakery. One of them tossed the flier away, and it landed at her feet. She picked it up and read the words out loud.

**"Opening soon: 'Sweet Bites' Free treats on opening day."**

She slowly shook her head as she gazed at the flier in her hand. Her head whipped up as the sound of a roaring car engine drew closer.

A man stepped out of a black Bentley that pulled to a halt in front of the new bakery and her gaze traveled up the building to see a sign with bold letters going up.

*'SWEET BITES'*

Lucy crumpled the flier in her hand and tossed it into the bin with one perfect throw. She looked back at the black-haired stranger who had gotten out of the car and was now staring at her. She noticed he had a smirk on his face that triggered a sickening feeling in the pit of her stomach.

*It seems I have new competition;* she thought as the dull ache spread through the rest of her body.

# EAT ONCE, DIE TWICE

AN IVY CREEK COZY MYSTERY

## RUTH BAKER

ALSO BY RUTH BAKER

**The Ivy Creek Cozy Mystery Series**

Which Pie Goes with Murder? (Book 1)

Twinkle, Twinkle, Deadly Sprinkles (Book 2)

Waffles and Scuffles (Book 3)

Silent Night, Unholy Bites (Book 4)

Waffles and Scuffles (Book 5)

Printed in Great Britain
by Amazon

21783596R00066